MW01328029

AS DEEP AS THE OCEAN

CINDY CALDWELL

Although this book is fiction, the imminent extinction of the tiny vaquita porpoise is not. If you'd like to learn more about them, you can do that here. This book is dedicated to the vaquita in hopes that they will survive.

ONE

Cassie's stomach was a jumble of knots as she left her office at the Scripp's Institute of Oceanography in San Diego and slammed the door behind her. It had taken all the restraint she had to maintain her composure when her research project manager said what he had been avoiding for at least half an hour.

"How's your research going on the vaquita dolphin?" Daniel had asked, finally getting to the point.

Cassie rolled her eyes. Daniel knew they weren't dolphin, although they looked like them. They were much smaller, and were porpoises. "How many times do I have to tell you they're not dolphin, they're porpoise?"

Daniel laughed. "I'm just kidding. I know they're not dolphin. You really need to lighten up," he said, but she noticed he took a nervous glance at her out of the corner of his eye.

They had been working together for several years, searching for solutions to save the endangered porpoise living only in the Sea of Cortez in Baja California, and she knew him well enough to know he was struggling with something.

"You know exactly how things are going," she said, her eyes narrowing. "We start preparations on the breeding sanctuary next week. What's up?"

"I may as well just come out and say it. Please try to stay calm, Cassie."

She moved to the edge of her seat, grabbing her long blond hair into a ponytail at the back of her neck, her green eyes flashing. "Please, just tell me. You're making whatever it is worse."

Leaning back in his chair, Daniel rubbed his eyes with both thumbs. "The resort has declined our request for delay and assessment. They're going forward."

She jumped up, leaning over his desk, unable to stop herself. "Are you kidding me? When did that happen? Why? How could they?" Her voice shook with fury, and she sat back down with a thud. "The government already approved it. It was all set."

"My thought is the owners of this resort are further up the food chain than we thought. And there's more."

Shaking her head, she stared at Daniel. She had to be dreaming. Her heart ached as she thought of her life's work going up in flames, or drowning in the ocean. Neither one was good. "More?" she asked.

"The owners have rescinded their offer of water rights for the sanctuary."

It wasn't often Cassie Lewis was speechless. Her reputation for fiery indignation was legendary at the Institute. Even with such a passionate group of researchers, her efforts on behalf of Baja sea creatures had gotten her in more fixes than she could count.

She found her voice, riddling Daniel with questions. "Don't they know the vaquita are almost extinct after all these decades of overfishing?

"Our report asking for a delay was complete and explicit, Cassie. You did a great job on it, all hundred and fifty pages."

He dropped the report on the desk with a thud. All those long nights in the library, and days on the water in Mexico, researching what was in those pages, worthless. Even now, though, losing the small porpoises to their imminent extinction was not an option she was willing to consider. "What can I do, Daniel? Who can I talk to? Who made this decision? Why don't they want to do what's right?"

Daniel sighed deeply. "I don't know the answers to any of those questions, Cassie. You're the best marine biologist I know, but that may not be enough. All I know is what I received from the Mexican government, and from the resort owners. We're out, they're in."

Cassie put her head down on Daniel's desk,

fighting back tears. She'd spent an entire year researching where along the white sand beaches it was feasible to create a small, protected space to help the vaquita stay out of harm's way—out of illegal fishing nets—and hopefully help their numbers grow. She had hoped, like most projects in Baja California, the five-star resort planned at Rancho Del Sol was just a pie-in-the-sky idea of some wealthy investors from Mexico City.

But it wasn't, and it had taken months of pestering the parent company to agree to set aside several miles of coastline for the sanctuary and when they finally had after months of delicate negotiations, with the additional agreement of the government, they'd been ecstatic. This was the only place that had ticked off all the boxes of suitability and they'd celebrated for days when the owners and the government had consented.

Now, her mentor dropped this bombshell on her.

"Cassie, we can start from scratch. Find another place. This one's going nowhere."

She shook her head. "You know as well as I do with the numbers of vaquita as low as they are and the fishing continuing, there's no time. No time at all. We can't start over, Daniel."

"Well, then, I guess it's over."

Cassie sat down slowly, her hand brushing over the cool cover of the report she'd worked on, slaved over. It was proof, in black and white, that there was soon to be another extinct species.

Daniel's voice interrupted her thoughts, her heart still pounding. "They did invite us to a groundbreaking celebration there next week, I think out of pity. If you can call it a celebration." He winced, handing her the invitation he had received.

Cassie reached out slowly and took the invitation from Daniel, running her thumb over the raised gold letters. Hot, angry tears sprung from nowhere as she read the invitation. Ribbon-cutting, cocktail reception, blah blah blah. Didn't they know they were not only going to ruin the chances of the vaquita surviving, but ruining the beautiful beach where she'd taken every vacation she had in her entire life? And it wasn't only the vaquita that would disappear—the area was home to sea turtles, hundreds of unique fish species and had the best shells for beach-combers anywhere, to her mind.

"I want to go," she said finally. "Maybe they'll listen to reason if I talk to them in person."

"I figured you'd say that," Daniel said, reaching behind him and taking an envelope out of a file folder. "I went ahead and notified their management that you'd like to speak at the press conference. You might not be able to change their minds, but I knew you'd want to make a public plea if it was possible. You're on the program. Fifteen minutes was all I could get you."

She nodded gratefully. "Thank you, Daniel."

He nodded in return. "You're welcome, but I'm not

remotely hopeful and you shouldn't be, either. There wasn't even a hint of wiggle room in the notifications. I know how much you've invested your heart in this, but you really need to admit it's not going to happen. Not here, anyway."

She blinked at him a few times before she shoved the invitation in her pocket.

"I had fiscal draw up the paperwork and approve the funds. I'm sorry, Cassie. Do you want me to go with you?"

"No, thanks," she said, shaking her head slowly. "I'll get somebody to go. I know you've got a presentation next week."

"I do, but I'd cancel it if you wanted me to."

"Thank you," she said. "I'm very grateful for everything you've done for the vaquita—for me. I'm determined to do whatever I can to make them understand how urgent this is, and I'm certain I can make them change their minds."

Daniel shoved his hands in his pockets and smiled, shrugging his shoulders. "I wouldn't get your hopes up, but If anybody can, you can. Oh, and you've got tons of time off. Why don't you just go tomorrow and maybe get a little R & R out of it. Take some deep breaths. Think about what you're going to say."

"Thanks, Daniel. I really appreciate it." She picked up the report and threw her purse over her shoulder.

"I'm sorry, Cass. I really am," Daniel said.

"Me, too," she said before she closed the door of his

office behind her. She still wasn't sure how this could have happened. She'd been so careful, and positive she'd had all her ducks in a row. She couldn't imagine what had thrown everything sideways so late in the game, but she held the report tight to her chest as she fished for her car keys. All she knew was she would find out and do anything she could to change it.

TWO

The sun had just set behind the skyscraper across from the Costa Azul headquarters. Alex Vasquez stood in front of the floor-to-ceiling windows of his penthouse office and waited for the last glimpse of the sun to fade. As it did, lights flicked on in the office buildings, illuminating the tall buildings.

He turned back toward his desk, settling in the high-backed black leather chair. He thought he might be able to tackle a few more things on his to-do list, but as he reached for the engraved invitation his PR department had set on his desk for the ribbon-cutting ceremony next week in Baja California, he couldn't help but let his mind wander.

It was a beautiful property, one that had been in his family for generations. He'd honestly never thought that they'd build a resort on it, as his family had also, for generations, vacationed there. He knew his mother and her family had had a vacation home there, although he hadn't been there since he was a young child and his memory had faded as to what it looked like. He'd hoped they'd spend much time there —swimming in the Sea of Cortez, collecting shells along the beach and his father teaching him how to fish —but after one particular trip, they'd never returned. Nor had it ever been spoken of again.

Until plans had been drawn up for the resort. His father had pronounced definitively in a board meeting several years ago that, "It was time." His mother had blanched and Alex himself had been confused, but the conversation between the two had ended with his mother silently nodding in agreement. It was just one mystery he'd chosen not to pursue in the family business he'd inherited as CEO. He just kept his head down and did his job, and if his family wanted a resort in Baja California to rival the ones they'd produced in Cancun and Cabo San Lucas, it was his job to make it happen.

He turned to the wall of framed photographs of every property they'd developed. He'd been proud of them all—not only did they work hard to maximize the beauty of the landscape, the views, but also to minimize the impact on the land. They did only what was necessary, and as he gazed at the pictures of the beaches at the resorts, he knew he'd done the best he could to protect them.

He loved his job—mostly—and as he'd been able to spend more time at the beach, on the ocean, he knew that this was something he cared deeply about. Every property they'd developed had been with the intention of a light footprint on the land, almost ECO-friendly if that was at all possible. They'd always made it a point to work hand-in-glove with the local communities and government, and assist in any way they could to ensure they would be welcome, and could give the eventual guests at their properties an opportunity to savor, yet respect, the natural beauty of the property. So when his mother had come into his office earlier and told him that the sanctuary requested by the Scripp's Institute of Oceanography was off the table, he'd been more than a little surprised.

Especially when he'd asked a question and his mother held up her hand to stop him.

"Alex, this is not negotiable. I realize that you are CEO but I remain president of the board, and we have decided. That beach will remain untouched, and will not become anything. Nothing at all. I've notified the government and they agree to rescind any permits. I have notified the Institute. It's all been taken care of, and I do not wish to speak of it again."

With that, she literally clutched the pearls she always wore and turned on her very expensive heals, her equally expensive designer suit flipping behind her as she rushed out the door as quickly as she'd come in.

"What was that about?" his friend and current

architect Raul said as he came through the door and leaned to watch Mrs. Vasquez turn the corner before he shut the door.

"Got me," Alex said as he fell into his executive chair and turned toward the view of the skyline.

"Did she say no vaquita sanctuary? We've built it into all of our models. It's part of the resort community physically, not to mention in all of our marketing plans. It would cost a fortune to change now. People will love it."

Alex laughed as he turned back around, his arms folded. "Your concern for saving a species from extinction is heart-warming, Raul."

Pink crept up from his friend's collar and he looked down, shuffling the papers in his hands. "You know what I mean."

Alex nodded. "Yes, I do. I really do. I hoped that this small compromise would work both to the Institute's advantage and ours. But it seems it's not to be."

Raul nudged his friend. "I see that keeping a species from extinction is first and foremost in your mind as well, my friend."

They both laughed and Alex reached for the report he'd reviewed before granting the request for the sanctuary.

"Yes, I see your point. It is disappointing, but I'm not sure we're remotely as disappointed as this young lady will be. It's quite a persuasive document they submitted."

Raul sat in the chair opposite Alex's desk, its soft and worn leather squeaking. "I'm glad I wasn't the one who had to break it to them. In fact, I'm glad I was in a different country when they found out."

"Coward," Alex replied.

"It's not like you told them yourself. I don't think anybody would want to crush someone's hopes and dreams like that. I certainly wouldn't."

Alex reached out for the bronze statue of two jumping dolphins that the Institute had sent along with the report. "Neither would I. Thank goodness for communications professionals."

"Right," Raul said as he laced his hands behind his head and stretched. "Why'd your mom put the brakes on it, anyway? What does she care?"

Alex stared at the closed door. He honestly couldn't answer that question. She'd seemed agitated, upset, and her eyes were red as if she'd been crying, now that he thought about it. He couldn't begin to imagine why she'd care about something like that, but in a traditional, Latin family there was no way he could even considering asking her. It just wasn't done. Even though he'd been to high school and college in the United States, he'd chosen to come home to work for—and with—his traditional family, and that's just how it was. He'd accepted it long ago and wasn't about to change now.

"I don't know, Raul. But something would have to

be more important than this to risk the wrath of my mother. And this just isn't worth it."

"Are you sure?" Raul asked, resting his elbows on Alex's mahogany desk. "Blood may be thicker than water, but not at the expense of your own destiny."

"Easy for you to say, my friend," Alex said.

Raul sighed. "I've got some changes to make on the plans before the ground-breaking and it would really help if I could visit the property again. You've only seen it once. How about if we go early and check things out? Boots on the ground. Besides, it's spring and the weather on the beach should be awesome."

Alex turned back to the view of the skyline. He'd been working so hard for years that he hadn't been out of the city in—well, he couldn't even remember. It might be good to take some time off before everything hit the fan in a week. He couldn't imagine that the Institute—especially that marine biologist—would be thrilled with them.

"All right. I'll put the pilots on notice that we're leaving tomorrow morning, first thing."

Raul pumped his fist and smiled. "Great," he said as he rolled up his drawings on the table and eased them into a hard case. "Don't forget your swimsuit," he said as he headed out the door, his smile even broader. "I hear the beaches are amazing. And teeming with lovely young ladies."

Alex shook his head as his childhood friend closed

the door. Lovely young ladies were the last thing he was interested in, but it had been a long time since he'd been at the beach, on the water. He missed it, and he might as well take advantage of this opportunity before it all turned into a dumpster fire.

THREE

Cassie reached her car, grabbed her phone from her purse and dialed her best friend, Taylor. They'd been traveling to Playa Luna in Baja California together as long as she could remember with their parents—now just their moms as both their dads were out of the picture—and their parents had frequently joked Cassie and Taylor had been friends since before they were born.

"Hey, Cassie, what's up," Taylor asked, her usual cheery greeting. Cassie plunked herself down on the curb of the Institute's parking lot. Hot tears burning her eyes, she gave her friend the bad news.

"Oh, Cassie, you're kidding me? That's awful," Taylor said, her voice low.

"I need to be there at the news conference. I have to stop this," she said, the back of her hand wiping her wet cheeks.

"I've got vacation time saved, and we're quiet right now. Want a wing-man? Might as well make a trip out of it." Her voice softened, and she said, "I know you'll figure something out, Cassie. You always do."

Cassie breathed a bit better, having made the arrangements to go. The relief was short-lived, though, and that night sleep didn't come. She played different scenarios over in her mind, trying to convince the developers the sanctuary was a necessary part of the future of Baja.

She thought of Playa Luna and felt a shiver of dread, wondering if she'd be able to help the vaquita. As the sun peeked through the windows, she gave up all hope of sleep. She packed a quick bag and was ready at the door at six a.m. when Taylor arrived.

"I've got all the supplies, Cass. All the road trip prerequisites," Taylor said as Cassie got into the car, pointing to the ice chest in the back. "All the stuff our parents always brought for Baja only. Remember? The stuff they wouldn't ever let us eat at home."

Cassie laughed as she opened the ice chest and saw the Red Bulls, Cokes and various chips. Nacho Cheese Doritos, Cheetos—and Taylor's favorite, Slim Jim's. "Oh, my God, when was the last time you ate a Slim Jim?" Cassie asked, shoving her friend's shoulder. "Your mom would kill you."

"Hey, I'm almost thirty. When do you get to eat what you want? And she doesn't know what I eat anymore. But you know as well as I do she'd do the same for a road trip to Baja," Taylor said, pulling onto Highway 8 toward the border, out of San Diego. "What happens in Baja—" she said with a laugh.

Passing through the California desert and over the border into Baja, they navigated the busy streets of the border town. Back in the desert for the desolate drive to San Felipe, the closest town to Playa Luna, Taylor broached the subject they had been avoiding.

"So, what are your plans, Cassie? How are you going to change this? It's a giant corporation, from what I read on the internet. Insanely rich family with ties to the government. They've even gotten family investors from Spain in on this one," Taylor said with a quizzical glance toward her passenger.

Still groggy from napping through the desert, Cassie's eyes hardened as the memory of her predicament returned. "I don't know, friend. I keep hoping for an idea, but it hasn't come to me yet. I know enough to know I can't just barge in there and demand they see the vaquita the way I do. I'm hoping to come up with something a little more—"

"Subtle?" Taylor chuckled.

With a smile, Cassie's eyes sparkled. "I've not been known to be exactly subtle."

"You think?" Taylor responded, laughing loudly. "I have faith you will come up with the perfect thing, Cassie," Taylor said, her voice softening.

They both fell silent as they came into the fishing town of San Felipe, the last vestige of true civilization before they reached their destination. They drove down its malecon, the main street along the beach, just for old time's sake. They stopped at the last mercado and stocked up on supplies—they'd need regular food besides the road trip items. "Want to stop for a taco?" Taylor asked.

Colorful blankets, hats, shirts and bathing suit cover-ups billowed in the breeze. Street carts full of shrimp and fish dotted every empty space. Laughter was everywhere, and Cassie sighed as the sun shone warm on her face, her tense muscles relaxing in the warm breeze.

"I'm okay if we just head down," Cassie said, eyes turning south. The sand and sea beckoned, her thoughts drawn again to the vaquita.

"Suit yourself, crazy woman," Taylor said, turning down the highway that was the last leg of the trip.

The last twenty miles of road meandered close to the water and again out into the desert. They passed the Valle de Gigantes, the strange and singular spot in northern Baja filled with Saguaro cactuses over forty feet tall. "Remember when we went there when we were little and you hugged the Saguaro, like a Redwood, and wanted me to take a picture?" Cassie asked. "Not your finest moment."

Taylor groaned and rolled her eyes. "Yeah. Thanks for helping me pick all the needles out the entire trip," She rubbed her hand over her arm at the memory.

Small dots of houses appeared as they drove

further toward Playa Luna. The motley group of communities—the south campos—stretched for over thirty miles along the coast of the Sea of Cortez, solar panels glinting in the sun. They were like individual neighborhoods, each with their own colorful signs, interesting inhabitants and personalities.

Halfway toward their camp, they passed Shell Beach and Rancho Del Sol, its mile-long dirt road leading to a small resort with cabanas and palapas covered in palm fronds providing shade for travelers and vacationers. This was the rancho that the company had bought and planned to develop into something monstrous, and she averted her eyes.

At its center was a lagoon full, most of the time, of treacherous mud.

"Remember when we rode up there on the four-wheelers and got stuck?" Cassie asked Taylor, her head out the window and the wind blowing through her blonde hair. She even loved the smell here, salt and sea spray in the air.

"Okay, another of my worst moments. Thanks for reminding me," Taylor said with a smile.

Older and wiser now, they were on another adventure. Turning down the dirt road to their camp, they rolled into the dirt drive.

"Woo-hoo," they said together, throwing the bags out of the car. They opened up the house that Cassie's mom had bought decades before, when Cassie and Taylor were babies. They'd already decided that

Taylor wouldn't even bother to open up her house across the dirt road behind Cassie's as there was plenty of room for both of them in the brick house on the beach.

"Gosh, it's good to be here." Taylor said. "Doesn't seem the same without our moms here to beat at Scrabble."

Cassie carried her bag into one of the bedrooms, glancing at the fire brick walls and opening the sliding glass door to let in the sea breeze. She inhaled deeply, and memories of her childhood in this place flooded in. Cassie and Taylor's mothers were best friends, and they'd all spent many happy times in this house and on this beach.

Taylor plopped her bag in one of the other bedrooms and carried in the ice chest from the car. "Have you talked to her yet? Told her what's happening?"

"No," Cassie said as she opened the cupboards in the kitchen to assess what was there. Opening a vacation house after having been away a long time was always a surprise. "I thought I should wait until I calmed down a bit and knew what my plan was. She'd just worry and get down here as fast as she could, and I know it's not a good time for her. I wish she'd retire, but right now she's really busy.

"She's not going to like that," Taylor said, glancing at her friend out of the corner of her eye."

"I know. But I think it's best. I'm worried about her."

"All right, if you think so," Taylor said. "I'm just glad you wanted me to come with you. I've worked so hard these past couple of years, and going into an MBA program will keep me at high rpm's for another two," Taylor said. "I sure needed a vacation, and you needed to get out of town, too. You've been burning the candle at both ends for way too long."

Cassie sighed and moved to set her clothes in the dresser. Their focus turned to the house, and the task at hand. A beautiful fire-brick house on a cliff overlooking the sea, it had been a place of respite for the two of them since they were children. They always thought of themselves as girl adventurers when they went alone, without their parents, as they had to remember how to "open" an all-solar house. Living off the grid as everyone did in the south campos, there was a bit to do before they could relax.

"Let's have a beer and relax before we start everything on the house," Taylor said, handing Cassie an ice-cold Corona, fresh out of the ice chest. Cassie grasped the icy bottle, taking a big gulp, and felt the cool, bitter liquid cascade down her throat, a flood of memories coming with it. She wasn't much of a drinker, but a beer on the beach? Oh, yeah. She wasn't going to pass that up.

"Ah, the beach," she said to Taylor, who wore the same contented smile Cassie did as they sat on the cliff and looked out to the water, listening to the waves crash against the shore.

Cassie and Taylor made quick work of igniting the water heater, lighting the old Servel propane refrigerator and making sure the water was flowing. They worked as a team on auto-pilot as they had many times before, completing the checklist with a fully operational house. They plunked onto their beach chairs, pleased with their work.

Pointing her thumb to the short road that would lead them there, Cassie asked, "Want to head down to the beach?"

"I know you want to check if you can see any vaquita, Cass, but I think a short siesta is in order for me. I drove, remember? You napped," Taylor said with a roll of her eyes.

Cassie smiled as her friend pulled out the hammock and set it up outside on the patio. Grabbing a chair and an umbrella, she said, "Suit yourself. I'm going to change and head down. I'll see you later."

FOUR

Alex pressed his thumbs to his eyes as he came out of a deep sleep. The hum of the jet engines had done him in shortly after takeoff. He leaned forward to look out the window, wondering how long he'd slept.

It had felt good. He didn't sleep much regularly when he was at home, and after his conversation with his mother the previous night, sleep had eluded him more than usual.

"Why do you want to visit early? I thought we'd agreed to fly in the day of the news conference and return the same evening. Just as we always do."

"Mother, the change in plans for the vaquita sanctuary will require some work by me and Raul. We thought maybe if we went early, we could have it all in place by the time of the news conference. He says we need to be boots on the ground. Why don't you come with us?"

He stiffened when his mother blanched. Her eyes grew wide, and she took a step back before she spoke.

"No. I have no desire to spend time on that beach—in that place. I will come in for the news conference, and that's all. You go if you want to, you and Raul."

She could be difficult sometimes, but overall she was reasonable, and he'd enjoyed his years working for the family company, earning his position as CEO. And in all that time, he'd never seen her quite like this.

He'd shaken his head at her obstinance, but still didn't want to rock the boat.

"Beautiful, isn't it?" Raul said from his overstuffed leather chair on the opposite side of the company jet's cabin.

Alex peered out his own window, blinking as the sun reflected off the blue water of the Sea of Cortez. He could still see the mainland side of the sea, but it faded as they approached the peninsula of Baja California. Fishing boats of all sizes dotted the water, and as they reached lower altitudes, he could tell the difference between the larger shrimp boats and the smaller fishing boats, called pangas.

He watched as the jet descended and flew over the beach, and passed the property that would become Rancho Costa Azul.

As they crossed over, Raul gave him a running commentary. "And that right there, that little lagoon, is where the high-rises will be. The swimming pool will be behind it, and the tennis courts will be a little further south. Kind of where the beach is where the vaquita sanctuary will be—um, was going to be, I mean. Do you want to see? I can point it out—"

"No, thank you." Alex cut him off. He knew where it was on the map and he didn't need to see it, now that it wasn't going to exist, anyway.

As the pilot flew past the property and circled for a landing on the solitary landing strip, the company had engineered, Alex looked across the valley toward the towering mountains miles across the desert. Cactus were everywhere, and the beauty of the desert differed greatly from property he'd seen in a while. It was like Cabo San Lucas, but less tropical. Less green, mostly. But beautiful nonetheless. He could see why his father was eager to develop the property—although as he scouted the horizon, it appeared that there was no other civilization nearby.

As the plane circled, though, to the south there were small groups of what looked like homes, and maybe a tiny town—called a poblado—a bit further down the single paved road that went in a straight line from north to south. He'd read all of this in the assessment reports and had wondered at the time why the cost of the project would be on the relatively high side. Now, he knew. There were no gas stations, no infrastructure really to speak of. Just a road. They'd have to start from scratch even to generate electricity, which explained vividly the need for a wide expanse of solar panels.

"I suppose I didn't realize quite how remote this spot was. I haven't been here since I was a small child."

Raul practically vibrated out of his seat with enthusiasm.

"That's what I've been telling you. This is a golden opportunity to build a resort completely off grid. It's never been done before quite like this. If we can pull this off, and market this way, ECO-tourists and fishermen from all around the world will want to stay here. It will be a marvel of forward-thinking infrastructure."

Alex glanced over at his friend. "You've been talking about this since we were in college. I guess I wasn't paying enough attention with all the other things we've got going on. It's not exactly as if you have a choice here. It's in the middle of nowhere."

Raul narrowed his eyes. "That's the great part. Opening up the beauty of this area without spoiling the rest of it. The resort will be practically the only thing here."

"It won't be for long," Alex muttered under his breath, not wanting to spoil his friend's excitement. But he was certain that the people from the Scripps' Institute weren't the only ones who'd be unhappy with what they had planned here. And he wasn't looking forward to hearing about that, either.

It wasn't long after the wheels had touch ground that Alex and Raul were situated in a nice—if a bit primitive for Alex's taste—casita at the existing tiny resort, Rancho Del Sol. Its two bedrooms and enjoining kitchen looked somehow familiar to Alex, and he wondered if this was where his family stayed when he was young. That would have been when his grandfather brought property here. It was the only actual restaurant and motel in the vicinity and had a certain rustic—charm, if Alex had to admit it. Apparently, the famous Baja 1,000 off-road race came by here and stickers from various race crews covered an entire wall in the restaurant, he'd noticed when they checked in.

Alex looked out the window at the beach, the palm-frond-covered umbrellas and the colorful beach chairs. The fronds covering the palapas swayed in the wind, and the waves gently lapped at the shore. When they'd checked in, they'd rented a small jeep as Alex wanted to explore the property over the course of the week, but for now, it might be fun to drive down the beach.

"You don't need to ask me twice," Raul said as he headed to his bedroom to change.

Alex did the same, and before long they were in the Jeep headed toward the beach. Alex loved driving, and he didn't get to do it much back home. The car and driver were always ready to pick him up, or he would just walk if his destination was close enough. So he gripped the steering wheel and revved the engine as he and Raul surveyed the miles and miles of beach in both directions.

"Which way?"

Raul leaned forward and looked north, then south. "Well, we own three miles of beach in both directions. We need to check it all out, eventually. How about south for now? I noticed a lot of houses in that direction and I'd like to see what that's about."

Alex nodded at his project manager, who thankfully knew a lot more about the project than he did. He'd been a little hands-off with this as his parents didn't seem to be too interested—until recently—and he'd had lots of other irons in the fire. Turning the Jeep south, now, and feeling the wind in his hair and feeling the salt spray on his face, it suddenly seemed a much more interesting project than it ever had before.

FIVE

Cassie's head cleared on the short walk down to the beach. Her umbrella set up and her chair perched perfectly underneath it in the shade, she strolled to the shore, inhaling deeply. She scouted for shells on her way and tossed a few in her pocket. Finally, her toes tingling as they wriggled in the sand, she felt the cool water lap at her feet.

She looked up to the sound of mechanical music and smiled at the familiar sight of the Pina Colada truck approaching. The lime green truck with wide tires barreled down the beach, stopping at every group of people under colorful umbrellas, trying to make a sale.

The drinks were cool and sweet, served out of half a pineapple, and they were a tourist favorite. She considered herself a local, though, and would wait for a margarita or something later after she got back to the house. She jumped at the honk of the truck as it passed by, shaking her head and declining the offer.

She returned to her vigil, trying to spy a vaquita, when she heard the pina colada truck flagged down by two men speaking rapid Spanish. A bit down the beach, a tall man with wavy brown hair in swim trunks flagged down the truck as he and his friend walked over to buy a drink. Sleek and self-assured, he wasn't the usual beach guy she'd been used to down here. Definitely not a local.

Cassie lay down in the sand, its warmth seeping up into her bones. Her mind wandered, and she realized she hadn't had time to even look at a man in the past year, even if she had wanted to. She'd been so hell-bent on creating the vaquita sanctuary that all other things in her life had taken a back seat, relationships included.

As her breath moved in time with the waves, she listened to the voice of the man at the pina colada truck. It had a strong quality, but not overbearing. He was asking the vendor how he was doing, and what his life was like, seeming to be interested in the response.

In easy conversation, they joked about the changes in Baja, the decline of the number of fish, and the more frequent sightings of dead vaquita on the beach, caught in the gill nets of the over-eager fishermen. Her ears perked up at that, and she sat up, wanting to hear more.

As she turned toward the conversation, she realized

the man she had been eavesdropping on was looking directly at her and she quickly looked the other way. Her cheeks flushed as she flipped over onto her stomach, her head still facing away to give her time to stop blushing.

His unusual amber eyes and wavy brown hair, a little long, were handsome, yes. But the way he carried himself, the way he spoke kindly and respectfully to the vendors, had caught her attention. His friend looked different, too, like they'd be more at home on the beach in San Diego than here in this sleepy fishing village.

He took a sip of his drink, and Cassie caught his eye over the rim of the pineapple. Horrified he'd caught her watching him, her hand betrayed her and shot up to give a little wave.

Wave? Really? Cassie groaned. She really was rusty with men. Trying to forget about the absurd wave, she walked down to the beach to take a swim, wading into the warm and inviting water. She did what her father had taught her to do in these waters and shuffled her feet to scare away any stingrays that might be lurking.

She had the fleeting thought she may look ridiculous, but sting-rays had stung enough of her friends on this beach it was non-negotiable. She took the precaution. Stingrays were plentiful here and came in with the high tide. She often saw the holes they had made to rest in as she walked the beach at low tide, after they had gone. Some holes were up to three feet wide, and they left indentations in the sand where their tails had been.

It was fascinating to her you could tell when it was time for the stingray young. Then, there were some huge holes, showing enormous stingrays in the area, and lots of much smaller ones surrounding them, some as small as eight inches in diameter. She knew for a fact they were here, so she shuffled, hoping she didn't look too silly, adding insult to injury.

She surprised herself, moving with ease against the waves. It felt good to use her strong legs, and she savored every moment of being in the warm, clear water. She'd always been a strong swimmer, but it had been a long time. She'd spent most of the past few years on the shore or in the water on a panga, working on her vaquita plan.

Now waist-high in the water, she pushed off, swimming leisurely. Big waves were infrequent here on her beach, and she navigated the small ones today with ease. She was a strong swimmer and loved the feel of the warm water on her body. Swimming steadily, she could feel the tug of the tide pulling her with each wave.

As Cassie swam in the clear water, she saw something big glimmering on the sandy ocean floor. Amazing shells were common here, and she was an avid collector. She couldn't stop herself, and diving to double check, she saw the telltale black-and-white pattern of a murex shell, a big one. It looked like it was intact, not like some others she'd collected on the shore that had been broken down by bouncing on the high tide line. This one hadn't been beaten down by the tide and the rocks, and this was a great find.

She surfaced, took a deep breath and dove back down. She grabbed the shell and pushed off from the bottom toward the surface, her prize clutched tightly in her hands. She wanted to make sure it was an unoccupied, abandoned shell as soon as she could so as not to disturb its occupant, so she tried to touch bottom with her toes as soon as she thought she might be close enough.

She gained purchase on the soft sand and stood up. As she filled the shell with water before she looked at it, she drifted toward the beach. She peered inside, one eye shut, to see if there was anything squishy hiding from her somewhere deep in there. If there was, she'd have to leave the shell. Not negotiable, either. Only empty shells were fair game.

Shaking the shell next to her ear—something her brother had taught her to do, but she'd learned meant absolutely nothing—she moved closer to the beach, forgetting all about shuffling her feet to avoid the stingrays. Just as she looked up and realized how close she was to shore, reminding herself to shuffle, she realized that it was too late. She felt the barb before she saw the sting-ray scoot away, and pain instantly shot through her that felt like lightning, starting at her thigh.

Her leg buckled, and she fell into the water, flashes of light before her eyes.

She yelled underwater at the shock, salty water filling her mouth. With a combination of anger and surprise, she clawed for the surface, trying to get to air. Her head broke the surface, but her leg was no use to her, and all she could do was flail, trying to balance on her one good leg as waves crashed against her, topping her again and again. Try as she might, every time she stood on one leg the next crashing wave bowled her over.

It didn't help at all that she was furious with herself. She knew better. She should have been shuffling, and this had never happened to her before and shouldn't have happened now. As she coughed, blinded by the intense pain, she struggled to stay afloat. She thrashed about in the water, trying to find her balance in both her body and her mind, but some part of her brain realized it was a losing battle. As she willed her body to be still, tendrils of blood wisped in the surrounding water, and she knew it was hers.

Dimly, she heard a voice from behind her. "Be as still as you can."

She tried, but felt her leg pulsating with pain. An arm shot out and grabbed her around the waist, holding her head above water and moving along quickly. "Don't fight the waves. Just try to breathe until I get you to shore," she heard a man say.

It was all she could do to remain as limp as possible

and let him pull her in with the waves. She felt herself sitting on sand, still in the water, as he said, "Stingray?"

She nodded as she coughed and pointed to her thigh. The man searched her legs and when he saw the barb, he said, "Look, there's the pina colada truck again."

Cassie thought he might be insane, but she managed to turn and look up the beach for the pina colada truck at the same time as another stabbing pain ripped through her thigh.

She gasped and turned to the man, who looked apologetic but held up the barb of the stingray he'd just pulled out of her muscle.

"Better to do it in the water. Sit here for a moment while you catch your breath and the water will pull out some of the venom."

She struggled to get air into her lungs while getting water out as she nodded.

The man turned and sat down next to her. "I hope it was worth it," he said slowly, humor in his voice.

She looked over at him as her breath steadied and slowed. Her leg was still in agony, and she couldn't imagine what he might think was funny.

His eyes twinkling and his smile broad, he pointed to the murex shell clutched in her hands. She looked down at it, amazed. All of that, and she'd still kept the shell? She'd thought she'd dropped it long ago.

She couldn't help but laugh, too.

"Oh, good grief." She lifted it up and turned it around in the bright sunlight. "Yeah, maybe it was."

"Well, you're totally committed, I'll say that for you," he said as he stood and reached for her hand. He helped her up, but she wasn't able to put any weight on her injured leg, and as she hopped on her other foot, more pain shot through her in pulsing waves.

She'd only hopped twice when suddenly, with a swoosh, Cassie felt herself being carried back to the beach chair by the man who'd been at the pina colada truck earlier, and she was grateful he was holding her as she didn't think she could make it on her own.

As he set her carefully on the chair, Taylor arrived on the four-wheeler, skidding to a stop right before them. "Cassie, are you all right? I saw from the house you were struggling in the water. What happened? Is that blood?"

Cassie still couldn't speak, and the man directed Taylor to find some hydrogen peroxide and bandages as fast as she could, along with hot water. Normally, Taylor would have said something to the tune of, "Well, who the heck are you?" Mercifully, this time she didn't.

She hopped on the four-wheeler and headed back to the house as fast as it would go. Cassie felt as if time had stopped completely, the pain searing her leg and feeling as if it were pulsing through her entire body. Taylor appeared with what the man had asked for. She pulled Cassie's blonde hair away from her face and stroked her forehead with concern. "What the heck happened?" she asked the man, not taking her eyes off Cassie.

"A stingray got your friend. I already removed the barb, but we need to get it clean as quickly as possible. I'll need you to get some sea water over here," the man said, still holding Cassie's leg and reminding her to breathe.

Taylor quickly grabbed the only thing handy to transport water, the pineapple holding the pina colada. She rinsed it best she could and scooped up the salt water and, running as fast as she could without spilling it, returned to Cassie, handing over the water.

It was obvious the man knew what he was doing, first soaking Cassie's leg in salt water, then peroxide. He cut a bandage from the first aid kit Taylor had brought, pressing it against her thigh for a bit to stop the bleeding. As the pain began to fade, Cassie struggled to take in what had happened. She stared at her rescuer with gratitude.

"Who are you? How did you—how did you know how to do that?" Cassie stammered, still struggling through the fog in her head. With a gleaming smile, the man answered "I guess there hasn't been time to introduce myself. My name is Alejandro. Alex, to my friends. I was in the Mexican Navy, where we learned emergency first aid."

"It's a good thing you were here. I wouldn't have

known what to do except what they did one time on Friends when one of them was stung by a jellyfish."

Cassie, taking inventory of her senses, realized she had full use of her faculties again after the scare. Enough so, that is, to see Taylor standing behind the handsome stranger and give her a thumb's up, accompanied by a huge smile.

"Oh, no," she groaned. "I'm glad we didn't have to do that."

"Me, too," another man said as he walked up to them with a first aid kit in his hands. "I saw you rush over and thought we might need this. But I see someone beat me." He smiled at both Cassie and Taylor.

"And this is my friend Raul," Alex said, and Raul shook Taylor's hand with a big smile.

"I'm Taylor and this is Cassie, the wounded," Taylor said and Raul laughed.

"Thanks a lot. Not a title I want," Cassie said as she turned her gaze from her friend and onto the man who was gently tending her wound. Up close now, she looked at him more intently. About six feet tall, his wavy brown hair tumbled over his forehead, almost covering his amber eyes as he bent over Cassie with care.

Once again, he caught her eye as she looked up. He smiled and looked at her kindly. "I'm glad I was here. Right place at the right time," he said, with a tiny hint of a Spanish accent.

"I will need to clean the wound better, with more peroxide. And you really need to soak it in hot water for at least thirty minutes, preferably ninety," Alex added with a look of concern toward Cassie's red and swollen leg. "How are you doing? Are you breathing all right?"

Cassie turned her full attention to her rescuer and confirmed that, although the sting still hurt, her breathing was fine.

Alex was methodical and gentle as he cleaned the gouge on her leg. Cassie was pretty good with blood and all things medical, but she felt herself starting to get dizzy as the pain increased. She grabbed the sides of the chair, squeezing so hard her knuckles turned white.

"Hey, you're hurting her," Taylor said, jumping over to Cassie's side and grabbing her hand. "Here, Cass, grab onto my hand and squeeze. I can take it."

"I'm sorry, ladies, but it has to be done," Alex said, continuing on with his work. "If I don't do this, it will be a lot worse before it gets better."

"It's okay, Taylor, I can take it," Cassie said, meekly for her. She was usually so strong, but this was a level of pain she had never experienced before.

Alex smiled, too.

"I'm fine, really. You don't have to do that," she said, shaking off her thoughts.

"You're not fine. Not quite yet," he said firmly.

Slowly, he turned her leg this way and that,

checking to make sure he had cleaned the wound thoroughly. Taylor held her hand the entire time, which seemed to Cassie to take days, not minutes. She let herself squeeze Taylor's hand when it hurt the most, remembering Taylor had performed this service for her own mother when she was in chemotherapy, having blood drawn almost every day. Her mom had been afraid of needles and Taylor stepped up to the challenge of comfort and providing broad shoulders. Cassie was grateful to have her best friend with her while she did everything she could to stay calm.

As Alex finished up, Cassie felt the blood returning to her head. She could sit up, finally, and was curious to see the red gouge in her thigh. Instinct caused her to reach out to touch it, and he grabbed her hand midway to her thigh. "Don't. We need to bandage it properly to make sure it stays as clean as possible," he said, looking over the wound seriously.

Alex, surveying his handiwork, seemed satisfied. "I'm pretty sure we got everything out that needed to come out. I hope I didn't hurt you too badly." He seemed genuinely concerned he hadn't hurt her too much.

Cassie looked at her leg, up at him, and back to her leg. She seemed unable to form a sentence.

"Uh, she—we—are really grateful. I'm sure it's fine," Taylor said, chiming in as her friend didn't respond. With a quizzical look at Cassie, she said, "I don't know how she would have made it to shore if you hadn't been right there." Cassie gave her friend a grateful glance for filling the dead air. Taylor winked at Cassie, and said to Alex, "So now what do we do, Captain?"

Alex smiled at the term, and quickly replied, "I'm no captain. Just a lucky guy with some skills that came in handy. And I would never pass up an opportunity to save a damsel in distress," he said with a grin. So, he's humble, too, thought Cassie, and funny.

"We should probably get you back to your house now, and out of this sun." Alex looked up the beach toward the houses on the cliff. "Where, exactly, is that?" he asked, sounding a little puzzled.

Cassie was glad Taylor had had the presence of mind during all the drama to switch the quad for the jeep permanently stored in Cassie's parents' garage. It wouldn't be the first time the car had gotten them home safely during an adventure. "We can take the jeep," Taylor said, tilting her head in the direction of the four-wheel drive vehicle. "It's the house right up there, just around the bend," she said, pointing out the brick house with the arches standing on the cliff. "You have to go up to it from the back, but it's easy. I'll show you."

Raul helped Taylor pick up all the supplies and hustled over to the jeep, placing everything in the back. She opened both of the front doors for Alex and waited for them to join her for the ride up to the house.

"I'll follow," Raul said as he hopped into a red Jeep.

Cassie braced herself to stand, hoping she could hobble over to the Jeep without falling flat in the sand. She gasped when, rather than let her get up and try her weight on her leg, Alex swept her up into his arms, carefully avoiding the wound. He set Cassie in the passenger seat, taking great care not to let her leg brush against anything that would hurt her in any way. Cassie melted into the seat, once again grateful for friends, new and old.

SIX

"I'll sit in the back," Taylor said. "You drive, Alex, and I'll show you where to go."

He hopped into the jeep and turned the engine over. With great skill, he traveled through the deep sand, avoiding any big dips or bumps. The short ride to the house was as gentle as it could have been, given the size of the sand dunes and the need for 4-wheel drive.

Pulling up to the house, he switched off the ignition, turned to Taylor and said, "Can you get some more bandages?" To Cassie, he said, "Stay put."

He came around to the passenger side of the car, retrieving Cassie once again, and carried her inside. He scanned the house and walked into the bedroom, bending slowly as he placed her on the bed. He stood nearby while they waited for Taylor, Raul and the supplies, glancing at his surroundings.

"How are you feeling?" he asked cautiously.

"I think it's getting better," she said, amazed her tongue was no longer glued to the roof of her mouth. "You did a wonderful job. I don't know what I would have done without you."

"Thanks for letting me out of the jeep, Tarzan. I had to crawl over the seats and out the window," Taylor said, with a gleam in her eye. "Not sure I would have made it without Raul. Guess you were in a hurry."

"Oh, sorry about that. I was in a hurry to get your friend comfortable," he said.

"I'm so sorry for all the trouble. I can't believe that this happened—I know better. I should have been shuffling."

Alex was still looking at her steadily. Cassie wondered what he was thinking, but didn't have the courage to ask.

"I can't believe you didn't shuffle. Your mother would have a fit. For that matter, my mother would, too," Taylor said, shaking her finger at her friend.

Taylor set the supplies on the nightstand, breaking the hush hanging over the room. Neither Cassie nor Alex noticed she had brought in the pineapple, too, that had saved the day. She did notice, however, a commotion out in the living room heading her way.

In a flash, a big black ball had bounded past Alex and jumped on the bed. Cassie screeched as Taylor leapt toward the bed, grabbing at the dog with one hand and the lamp with the other. "Whiskers, no!"

Taylor shouted and she steered the panting dog onto the floor.

"Thanks for getting to him before he got to my leg," Cassie said, smiling at Taylor. Turning to the black, disheveled mutt, she smiled and said, "Hi, Whiskers. You worried about me?" Whiskers gave a little whine and sat on the floor, waiting for Cassie or Taylor to give him permission to return.

"Jimmy must be nearby," Taylor laughed, glancing out the door looking for the dog's owner. Whiskers only turned up if it was somewhere Jimmy was going. One of the longest residents of Playa Luna, Jimmy was a bit of a misfit, and there was much speculation why he'd chosen to live most his adult life in Mexico. He'd moved down to live with his parents over twenty years ago and had been to the United States only once during that time.

Poking his head in the door, Jimmy said, "Hey, ladies. What's up? Saw you had some trouble down at the beach." One good thing about having Jimmy around, Cassie thought, was if anything went wrong, he was always there to help. Sometimes she thought he was like a mother hen with all of them in camp. Nothing wrong with having an uncle to watch your back, though, so she said, "We're in here, Jimmy. This is Alex, and this is Raul. Alex, Raul, Jimmy Martin."

The three men shook hands and Jimmy glanced at Cassie's bandaged leg. "Accident?"

Taylor threw him a wry smile. Jimmy was a man of

few words, and usually short ones. "Yep," Taylor confirmed. "The Captain here saved her after she lost all ability to swim when the stingray barb got stuck in her leg."

Jimmy raised his eyebrows. "You weren't shuffling, were you, Cassie?"

Cassie groaned and realized she was never, ever going to live this down.

Jimmy inspected Alex, his eyes narrowed. "Captain?"

Alex lowered his eyes, holding his hands up in front of him. "No, not a Captain. I was in the Mexican Navy for a while, that's all. Just learned about first aid." He glanced at Taylor, and she wrinkled her nose at him and smiled.

"Well, it's a good thing you did," Jimmy said gruffly. He was a bit of a different sort. His long gray beard and piercing blue eyes made him look a little wild. And he always said exactly what he thought. "Thought you were a good swimmer, Cassie."

The air rushed out of Cassie's lungs and she reddened. He always could get to her. "I am, and you know it. I just got a little distracted when I was under trying to pick up a shell and I forgot what I was doing." She tried not to sound defensive. Grateful that someone had rescued her, she still wanted to keep her reputation as a competent, capable swimmer.

"Oh, you know how it is when you panic, Jimmy," Taylor added, hoping Jimmy would let it die.

"I've seen Navy divers panic during practice exercises and almost drown. No shame in being hit with a new situation and having it roll right over you," Alex said.

"Well, don't let it happen again," Jimmy said over his shoulder as he and Whiskers walked out of the room.

Taylor laughed after he'd gone. "Man, he's a tough one, isn't he?"

"And that's no exaggeration," Cassie added, grateful he'd gone, but equally grateful he'd checked in on her. It was familiar and comforting, and she didn't take offense.

"Is he always that gruff?" Alex asked.

"Yes. That was actually on the warm and fuzzy side for him," Taylor said. "Sorry Whiskers jumped on you. I couldn't get to him in time."

"No problem. He missed my leg," Cassie said, grateful yet again for small favors.

"This is quite an interesting campo you ladies have here. And this is quite a lovely house," Alex said, looking about the brick house with its arches and carefully matched Mexican firebrick. "I haven't seen whale-tail matching of this quality in a long time."

He explained to Taylor and Cassie how each set of bricks was fired in such a way they were an exact but opposite match. "It takes a skilled craftsman to do a job of this quality," he said, his eyes lingering over the handiwork. "They're called whale-tails. See how they sometimes look like the tail of a whale as it fans out of the water?" Cassie hadn't noticed before, but now could see them throughout the beautiful walls and patio.

"My mother said this house was built by a man who was in construction, a craftsman, who built only churches. This was the only house he ever built that wasn't a church, and he built it for his bride. She died shortly after and we bought it when I was little."

"Do you know his name? Or where he came from?"

Taylor looked at him, her eyebrows raised. "No, I don't, but I could try to find out. I do know he was despondent after his wife died, and he stayed in the south campos. My mother might know of him, or maybe Jimmy."

"Never mind," he said, turning back to Cassie. "It's not important. This young lady's health is paramount right now."

Cassie noticed he had been a bit flustered by that information. She would have loved to ask why, but Alex quickly cleared his throat and began to instruct the women on what to do next. "This is important, you two, if you want the pain to stop as soon as possible."

He sat on the side of the bed and slipped a gauze bandage around Cassie's leg, securing it tightly.

Turning to Cassie, he said, "That'll stop the bleeding. Soak your leg in a hot bath for at least thirty minutes. Ninety would be better. Make it as hot as you can stand, and the water will neutralize what's left of the venom. Then take some ibuprofen and get some rest." It pleased Cassie the directions sounded so simple. She looked forward to a bath in her favorite blue marble bathtub to rinse off the sand and salt.

He had delivered his instructions clearly and concisely, and he turned toward the door. On his way out, he stopped mid-stride and turned to Cassie. "It has been very nice to meet you both, even if under unfortunate circumstances.

Alex took the hand of each one of them and gave a slight bow, in the Mexican tradition. "Mucho gusto, Senoritas."

"It's very nice to meet you, too," Cassie said as Raul did the same, and even Taylor showed a little flush in her cheeks. "Thanks for this, for everything. I really owe you."

He smiled, his white teeth flashing and his eyes twinkling. "Think nothing of it. Any gentleman would do the same."

"Hey, why don't you guys come back for dinner? Cassie can just sit there with her leg up if she needs to, but we have stuff to make hamburgers. Plenty for all of us. Least we can do after you saved Cassie's life," Taylor said, winking at Cassie. "That's all right with you, Cassie, isn't it?"

Cassie's eyebrows rose as she glanced at her friend. If her leg wasn't sore and she was honest with herself, she definitely wanted to know more about Alex, his time in the Navy. He was interesting, and a bit mysterious.

"That would be great, if you can manage the cooking." Cassie was pretty positive she wouldn't be up for standing by a stove—or a barbecue.

His eyebrows shot up with surprise. Cassie had the immediate sense she may have been a bit too honest. She didn't really understand Mexican men all that well. She was an American girl through and through, and she hoped her invitation hadn't been a mistake.

"Are you certain you will feel up to it? I mean, after your injury?" he asked, glancing at the gauze wrapped around her leg.

Her pain was fading, and even though it still hurt, she was confident that she'd be up for dinner. If someone else made it.

"I think I'll be all right after a good soak. I definitely would like to thank you with dinner."

Alex nodded slowly. "I think I could manage that," Alex agreed with a shy grin. "We're staying at the Rancho Del Sol, and we can go clean up and return after you've had an opportunity to thoroughly soak your wound. It'll give me a chance to look at it later, too, and make sure there are no signs of infection."

Taylor and Cassie exchanged quick glances. "Perfect," Taylor said. "Hope you're all right with hamburgers and corn on the cob."

Raul chimed in with enthusiasm. "One of our

favorites. We went to school in the states and are big fans. We love hamburgers, don't we, Alex?"

All the arrangements were set.

"Absolutely." Alex started for the door behind Raul and took his leave of the two women with another slight bow.

His amber eyes bore down on Cassie. "I look forward to seeing you this evening. Get some rest," he said, as he headed out the door.

SEVEN

Raul hopped behind the wheel and Alex didn't mind at all, just sitting in the passenger seat and looking at the scenery as they drove north toward where they were staying. With the Sea of Cortez on his right, Alex looked at every house, either on a cliff or the beach as the terrain changed, as they drove along.

"That was eventful," Raul said after they'd passed the girls' house and waved.

Alex turned around in his seat after waving. "It sure was. I had no idea what was wrong in the beginning when Cassie was flailing, only that she was in distress."

"You sure got there in a hurry."

"As did you with medical supplies. Good teamwork."

Raul laughed. "Ever since we were kids, you

rushed in and I was on clean-up duty. I know what to do."

"I had to rush. She was in trouble." Alex glanced at his lifelong friend to see if he was teasing—and he was, as usual. Raul had a streak in him where he couldn't pass up a chance to get a dig in, and over the past few years that Alex had been working at the family business, he'd grown to count on it. It helped him take himself less seriously, and to remember to have fun.

"Yes, she needed help. And you were certainly rewarded with two grateful young ladies. Two beautiful, grateful young ladies, I might add."

"I would definitely agree."

"I'm surprised you noticed," Raul said with a wink.

Alex frowned. "Have I been out of commission that long?"

"Longer than long," Raul said. "It was nice to see you with a woman. You've been pretty pre-occupied for—what—a decade?"

"It hasn't been that long."

"It has," Raul replied.

"Look at those round houses. Made of that fire brick. They're interesting," Alex said in an effort to change the subject, and it worked. Raul was interested in anything and everything about construction, and passive energy, and Alex truly wanted to see what he thought.

"This is an unusual part of Baja. No electricity, no

community water, no sewer. Odd. Close enough to the border that Americans have been coming here to fish for almost fifty years. These people are locals as much as we are. And pretty hardy, at that. I don't know many people who would live with no water and no electricity. Although we are getting to where it can be much more do-able. I still hope that the board will be much more aggressive with renewable energy for this project."

"Actually, being here I can see why you'd think it was a perfect opportunity to experiment." Alex said as he turned back toward the sea.

"What's that?" Alex pointed to what looked like a speck in the distance.

Raul stopped the jeep and reached behind him, grabbing the tube of papers he always carried with him. He popped off the top and pulled out his drawings, spreading them out over the steering wheel as he got his bearings. He looked out toward the horizon and back to his drawings.

"It appears it is a small island, too small to inhabit. It's called Vaquita Island. I would venture to guess it's named after those small dolphins."

"Ah," Alex said, nodding. "And Rancho Del Sol, where we're staying, is what we will tear down to make way for the resort."

"Mm-hm." Raul pored over the plans and looked around. He pointed to the west. "Over there is where the tennis courts will go, and to the north of that is the golf course." He looked at Alex and smiled. "But you know that. It's your resort."

Alex had, in fact, gone over the plans multiple times but had never been to the site—at least not that he remembered. "Somehow, it looks spartan when you're here. It's very different from all of our other properties. It's mostly desert."

"Ah, yes, where the desert meets the sea," Raul replied, rolling his plans back up and placing them in their protective tube.

"Hm, yes. That's catchy—and true. People seem to love it here."

"Well, Cassie and Taylor sure do. And that old man—what was his name?"

"Jimmy, I think. Seems as if they've been coming here for a very long time."

Raul turned the engine over and started again up the beach. "Yes, and they all seem very attached. This will be a big change for them."

"It will," Alex said as he leaned back in the seat and closed his eyes. The sound of the waves and the warm sensation of the sun on his skin brought peace, and he could see why their new friends loved it here. Even with the harsh desert and prickly cacti, it had gentleness he couldn't remember experiencing anywhere else.

Raul soon pulled into Rancho Del Sol and Alex shook himself out of his thoughts.

"Want to grab a beer before we get ready for dinner?" he asked.

"Sure. I was thinking of asking the restaurant if there was anything we could get to take back down, so we don't show up empty-handed."

"Always the gentleman," Raul said, nudging his friend with an elbow.

Alex and Raul grabbed a table by the window, the ice cold beer they'd ordered arriving almost as soon as they took their seats.

"Salut," Alex said in a toast, and he nodded at the waitress as she delivered chips and salsa. "Would it be possible to order chips, salsa and guacamole to go," he asked, and the young lady smiled and nodded.

"Of course. I'll bring it right out."

They both sat quietly, watching the waves crash against the beach as fishermen came in with their catches of the day. Two older men, clearly American, trudged up the beach and came into the restaurant with an ice chest in tow, and the cook came out of the kitchen to meet them.

"Great catch today," the cook said as he took money from the cash register and traded the men for the fish—dorado and grouper, apparently, from what they were saying.

The fishermen crossed over to the bar and ordered two beers, giving up some of their recent income.

"Ah, this is the life, eh?"

His buddy agreed. "Sure is," he said as he took the ice cold beer that the bartender held out for him.

"Hey, did you see the big sign out there for the press conference about the resort? I can't believe it's really going to happen. That'll sure be a game-changer."

His friend nodded slowly. "I didn't think it would ever happen, either. At least I was hoping it wouldn't happen. Hey, Juan, how long before you think this joke will get going. It'll change everything down here."

"Not long, Señor," the bartender said, and Alex looked away as the man glanced in their direction. "They're planning to begin soon, from what I understand."

The other fisherman shook his head slowly. "You're right. I never thought I'd see the day. Was hoping it was on Baja time, if you know what I mean. Mañana. Tomorrow. Always tomorrow."

"All those letters we wrote, those petitions we signed. Nothing."

His friend turned around and rested his elbows on the bar. "You know it's always about money."

Raul and Alex exchanged glances. Raul leaned forward and whispered, "Do you remember letters and petitions?"

Alex nodded. "A long time ago, in the beginning. But the board decided to go ahead anyway, and it died down. Right about the time we agreed to donate the property and water rights for the vaquita sanctuary, now that I think about it."

"Well, they're not going to like the new change of plan."

Alex looked over toward the fishermen and the bartender who were happily in conversation about something different.

"No. No, they won't. Seems we aren't all that popular around here, and they don't even know who we are yet."

"That's an understatement," Raul said. "Good thing the girls don't know why we're here. I don't think they'd have invited us for dinner if they did."

"No, I don't think they would have either," Alex agreed. "All the more reason not to tell them. Not yet, anyway."

EIGHT

"How are you feeling?"

"I don't think I remember ever feeling that way when a man touched me."

"Well, that's nice, but I was referring to your leg," Taylor said with a laugh. "Sounds like he's fixed it right up for you."

Cassie's face flushed. "I thought you meant—"

"Never mind. Let's get you into the bathtub for that soak he wanted you to take," Taylor said as she guided Cassie into the marble bathroom. "You love this bathtub, anyway, and we can get you all spiffed up for tonight."

"I don't think spiffed up is required. It's just barbecued hamburgers." Cassie leaned on Taylor's shoulder as they moved toward the bathroom.

Taylor started the bath and added some Epsom salts. "Right. Okay. You just concentrate on your leg getting better. That was scary, and you've only got a few days to get better. Hopefully, there won't be any infection." Taylor's voice trailed off as she left the room, and Cassie dipped into the hot water.

Cassie allowed herself to daydream as the bath worked on her throbbing leg. The beautiful blue and white marble soothed her, and it wasn't long before she felt much better.

The aroma of coffee stirred her from her thoughts, and she struggled out of the tub.

"You need any help?" Taylor shouted from the kitchen.

Cassie pulled on a white tank top and soft, pink skirt and answered, "No, I got it."

By the time she made it to the kitchen, Taylor was slicing the last tomato for the burgers and had everything set out on the colorful tile counter.

"Wow, nice job," Cassie said, easing onto a stool opposite the sink.

"Thanks," Taylor said, her hands on her hips with a look of satisfaction. "I think it'd make your mom proud. Especially since you don't cook, stingray barb or not."

Cassie laughed. "Good thing you're here so we don't starve."

They both turned toward the door as Alex and Raul knocked, then entered bearing chips and salsa. They'd both clearly showered—Alex's hair was no longer full of sand—and they definitely had a Latin flair with their khakis and buttoned, embroidered shirts.

"Brought something for you," Alex said with a smile as he set the chips, salsa and guacamole on the counter.

"Thank you." Taylor nodded at Raul and said, "Care to help me light the barbecue?"

As Taylor and Raul headed out to the patio, Alex asked, "How are you feeling?" He took a seat next to Cassie.

"Better, thank you. It still hurts, but the bath helped a great deal. I had no idea that's what you were supposed to do."

He smiled gently and pointed to her leg. "May I?"

Cassie smiled and nodded, pulling up her skirt a little. She'd taken off the bandage after her bath as it had soaked through.

Alex narrowed his eyes and inspected the gouge. "It looks pretty good. A little red still, but it's not oozing. No sign of infection so far." He reached into his pocket and took out a tube of antibiotic ointment. He smiled up at her, his eyes gentle, before he said, "I hope this won't hurt, but with this and another bandage, I think you'll be in good shape."

Cassie nodded again but winced as his warm hand rubbed on the cool ointment. He finished quickly and wrapped gauze around it again, patting her knee when he finished.

"There you go."

She looked up at him gratefully as he stood and took a step back.

"I'm not sure how to thank you, Alex. We'd have been at a loss if you hadn't been there—and here now."

Alex cleared his throat and ran his hand through his dark, wavy hair. "I'm sure it would have worked out fine."

He held out his hand, and she took it, easing herself off the stool and following him out onto the patio. The sun would set soon, over the mountains behind them and the sea would change, the sky turning many different colors until the stars came out. It was Cassie's favorite time of day, and she'd never enjoyed it more than this evening, sitting with good friends.

"Look, an osprey and its baby," Taylor cried, pointing out over the cliff. They all watched as the larger bird circled the baby as it got its bearings. It wasn't very old and just learning to fly, and as the baby tired and began to sink toward the ground, the mother circled and came up below it, lifting it higher and giving it a bit of a rest.

"Never hurts to get a little help," Cassie said as she turned to Alex. He was mesmerized by the sight and had stood up and crossed the sand over to the edge of the cliff.

"She's helping the baby? To teach it how to fly?"

Cassie stood and walked out to the cliff's edge. "Yes. It's critical for their survival that the osprey young be able to navigate the changing direction of the gusts that come off the sea at sunrise and sunset. And that they understand the changing tide line."

"I imagine that's important for any bird," Alex said as he pointed to a group of seagulls converged together offshore.

"Here we go." Taylor rolled her eyes as she gestured for Raul to follow her into the house and announcing they were ready to start cooking.

"Not exactly. The seagulls are there in the water because there are a lot of fish congregating there, but they also eat carrion. Easy pickings, and it's called a boil. That's their job and they're also taught that at a young age."

"Carrion?" Alex scratched his forehead, his brow furrowed.

"Oh, sorry. Dead animals, or dead fish. The osprey, on the other hand, eat only live fish, so they have to dive for them. But they don't get into the water really, so they must be strong aviators. Completely different."

Alex turned to her, his amber eyes questioning. "I had no idea. So how, then do the osprey eat if they can't get wet?"

"Watch," she said, pointing to another osprey circling the fish boil. As the seagulls dove and jostled for position, the osprey came at them dead on, swooping in so just its feet touched the water.

"Wow," Alex said as the osprey rose from the water, a fish wriggling in its talons. "That's amazing. Like eagles."

Cassie nodded and smiled. "You're a quick study."

"And so glad you're here to listen so I don't have to." Taylor winked at Cassie as she came back onto the patio carrying a plate of burgers.

As Taylor and Raul laughed and cooked the burgers, Alex and Cassie sat out on the cliff, watching the wildlife. The tide was coming in, and Cassie waved as people walked by with their dogs, frequently throwing sticks out into the waves for the dogs to fetch. She told him about the tide, the clams they dug at the point to the south, the fishermen who launched their beaches in the mornings and came back with buckets full of fish for dinner.

"You sure know a lot about—well, everything around here," Alex finally said.

"And that's just the tip of the iceberg," Taylor said as she set the delicious-smelling burgers on the patio table and Cassie's stomach rumbled.

"Oops. Guess I haven't eaten much today," she said as Alex took her hand, pulling her up.

They all ate and laughed as the sun set, and the sky on the horizon changed from pink, to purple and finally to dark blue. Cassie lit the candles on the table as darkness fell and the stars began to sparkle overhead. The warm breeze had the candles dancing, and as the burgers disappeared, Cassie paused.

"I've been babbling. Sorry."

"Nah, not you," Taylor said, laughing.

Raul smiled and nodded at Cassie. "It's been fascinating hearing about Baja, and your time here. And your wealth of knowledge about marine and desert life is impressive."

Cassie had hoped she wasn't boring them and flushed at hearing she wasn't. She'd tried to keep it light, purposefully avoiding discussion of the vaquita as she didn't trust herself not to get emotional like she usually did.

"What about you two? What brings you here? I know you're staying at the rancho. You all on vacation?"

Cassie paused and glanced at Taylor as the two men exchanged glances, but hesitated to answer.

"Alex?" Raul finally said as he looked expectantly at his friend with a cocked eyebrow.

Cassie waited, a little confused. "Vacation?"

Alex closed his eyes and let out a huge breath. "Yes, vacation. A little work while we're here, but vacation."

Raul frowned, and Cassie assumed it was because they had to work while they were in such a beautiful place.

"Same with us," Taylor said. "Some rest and relaxation, but always work to be done."

Taylor stood to clear the table and Raul followed.

Alex helped Cassie up and gathered more dishes from the table, following the others into the kitchen. Cassie was sorry that the moment had passed. She wanted to know more about Alex. A lot more. But it would have to wait.

"Oh, no," Taylor cried just as Cassie came through the sliding glass door and the lights went off.

"Oh, no," Cassie echoed as she stood in the pitch black darkness.

"What happened?" Alex asked, and Cassie could dimly make him out against the counter.

"Hang on," Taylor said, and in a moment a flashlight turned on and seconds later she lit a big candle on the counter by the sink. "Guess we've got no electricity."

"Where's your inverter, and panel?" Raul asked, taking a flashlight that Taylor offered him.

Over dinner, they'd talked about the fact that the house, while beautiful, was limping along on its solar panels and batteries and it had been next on the list to upgrade it. This trip had been planned in a hurry, though, and they were just hoping that things would hold out until next trip.

Taylor led him to the back of the house and they disappeared around the corner.

Cassie smiled at Alex, his eyes dancing in the flickering candlelight. "Guess this is one of the things that happens when you're off the grid."

"I suppose so," he said. "It's very interesting."

"Interesting is a good word," Cassie said with a laugh.

"Fascinating, actually," Raul said as he and Taylor

came back into the kitchen. "A really interesting, old school take on solar panels and electricity."

"Probably. My parents put it together probably thirty years ago, long before my dad died. We've been keeping it going with spit and bubble gum, my mom says," Cassie said.

Raul laughed. "That is a very apt description. And that's what it looks like. But the batteries aren't even holding anything that the solar panels are feeding it. The wire's frayed and much too thin. You really need an overhaul."

Cassie and Taylor sighed in unison. "Well, we don't know how to do that."

"We do," Raul said, squaring his shoulders. "Or I do, I should say. Alex is great at helping. We did construction work during summers in high school. Learn the trade. And I've worked with solar and can help. Is there anywhere around here to get a new inverter, some upgraded equipment?"

"I think so," Cassie said slowly. "I can ask Jimmy in the morning. I really don't want to ask you for help on your vacation. We've already monopolized your time."

Taylor cleared her throat loudly as she glared at Cassie, her eyes wide. "If they want to help, that would be great. Otherwise, we're here for days in the dark. No cell phone charging, no nothing."

"Oh, right." Cassis scrunched her nose and looked at Alex. "You don't mind?"

"Of course not," Alex responded. "How could we leave two damsels in distress?"

Raul laughed. "Absolutely. We'll be back first thing in the morning with what supplies we can round up beforehand and go from there."

"You certain you'll be all right on your own tonight?"

Taylor laughed. "It won't be the first time we've played Scrabble by flashlight."

"Well, if we have anything to say about it, it will be your last," Raul said as he and Alex headed toward the door.

Alex turned and took Cassie's hand, holding it to his lips for a moment. "Thank you for a wonderful evening. I appreciate knowing so much more about Baja. Thank you."

Cassie flushed and was glad for the candlelight to make it. "You're welcome, and thank you for everything."

The girls waved from the cliff as Alex and Raul drove north on the beach.

"Well, that wasn't how I thought tonight would turn out," Taylor said as they went back inside.

"Me neither." Cassie flipped the light switch one more time in disbelief, but nothing happened.

Taylor handed Cassie a flashlight and blew out the candle. "I don't know about you, but I'm beat. I'll do the dishes in the morning."

"I should be able to do it," Cassie said, glancing at her leg. "I feel much better, but I'm beat, too."

"I bet. It's been a huge day." Taylor blew out the remaining candle and headed for her room.

"It has. And sounds like it'll be another huge day tomorrow."

NINE

Alex looked over at Cassie a few days later as she pulled her long, blonde hair into a ponytail and her green eyes danced. She was lovely even in work shorts and a t-shirt, and they'd laughed for days as Raul and Taylor bent over drawings and calculations, and Alex showed Cassie how to use a staple gun. He'd enjoyed getting to know her even better, and it felt good to swing a hammer again after so many years of suits and board rooms.

At the same time, though, the twinges of guilt for not telling her who he was grew more frequent. From the day they'd started on the project, people from the south campos had stopped by—old friends of Cassie and Taylor, and brought food, supplies, anything they'd needed. He'd gotten to know a few of the men, including the Mexican camp owners, and he was beginning to understand exactly why they all objected to the building of the resort. It threatened to completely change their way of life, everything they'd known and loved about the Baja for generations.

He'd thoroughly enjoyed Cassie's company, and it turned out they worked well together. Raul and Taylor were the brains of the project, but they did a good job of executing their assignments. At least they had until now.

"Ouch," Alex yelled, and dropped the hammer he'd just smashed his thumb with. He brought it to his mouth and tried to stem the bleeding.

"Oh, no," Cassie said, dropping her own hammer and running for the first aid kit. She returned in a flash and came toward him with a bandage and gauze.

"Here, let me see," she said, her eyes full of concern. She held the gauze on it tightly but gently. "Here, you hold it and I'll get some ice."

She reached past the lemonade they'd been drinking and filled a small baggy with ice, holding it on his thumb. Although it hurt badly, he knew it wasn't serious—it would just be really sore.

"I'm sorry," he said as he watched Cassie check if it was still bleeding. "I must have gotten distracted. Too much beautiful scenery in here."

Cassie looked up, perplexed and glanced around the room they were replacing the wiring in, and to be honest, there was nothing special about it. Just her.

He smiled as she turned a lovely shade of pink,

realizing what he'd meant. "Oh, goodness. Well, you'd better pay closer attention."

"I'll try," he said as he reached into the ice chest and handed her a lemonade.

"We're almost done, anyway." Cassie turned away quickly and reached for her hammer, securing the last bit of wire that Raul had assigned them. "We should be able to have the great light show soon," she said, sitting back down beside Alex.

"Good thing. I don't think I'll be good for much for a while. Maybe we should be on supper duty."

Cassie frowned. "I don't think that would be very appealing for anybody. Taylor's the cook around here."

"She and Raul have a few more hours hooking everything up. I say we give it a try. I used to cook with my grandmother, and although it's been a very long time, I think I can remember how to go to the store and buy carne asada to barbecue. If we're lucky, they'll have beans and rice already made. All it takes is a few tortillas and call it dinner."

Cassie stood and put all the tools back in the bucket they'd hauled around the house for several days. "Yes, the store at the poblado has all that, and it's great. Better than anything I could make. We'll need to return Jimmy's tools, and maybe we could invite him for dinner, too."

"I say we invite anybody who's helped. Make a fiesta out of it," Alex said, surprising himself. He didn't have much of a social life back in the city, but here, somehow, even though he hadn't been here long, he felt at home.

Raul confirmed that he'd be done before dark, and Cassie and Alex headed to the store for supplies, stopping at Jimmy's house on the way to drop off the tools.

"Oh, my," Alex said as they pulled up to a round hill on a bluff overlooking the ocean. The large, round boulders it was made with were interspersed with what looked like the bottom of wine bottles of many colors— blue, red, green and some yellow.

"That's a most interesting house," he said as he stepped out of the jeep and grabbed the bucket of tools and followed Cassie toward the house.

"It sure is. One-of-a-kind, that's for sure. He built it all on his own."

He followed her through the arched wooden door and whistled. "Wow. This is fascinating." He glanced around and the inside was as unique as the outside. The place was small, but had a fireplace, a huge Mexican-tile sink and windows that looked out over the sea and on the other side, a magnificent view of the mountains.

"Doesn't look like he's here. I'll leave a note," Cassie said as she grabbed a pencil and jotted quickly.

They continued on the dirt road onto the highway he'd seen from the jet—which seemed like a lifetime ago. They ordered enough meat to feed an army, and Cassie gathered the other things. He noticed a bin of corn on the cob and remembered how his grandmother had cooked it when he was young.

"Have you ever had elotes?" he asked Cassie as he set their items by the cash register.

"Street corn? Yes, I love it."

He filled a bag with corn and grabbed some cheese out of the refrigerator, positive he'd seen the rest of the things he'd need back at the house.

When they got back, Raul confirmed just another hour or so, and Alex and Cassie got to work in the kitchen.

"You may not know how to cook, but you're good at heating things up," Alex said, and he smiled as Cassie wrinkled her nose. She did it often, and he thought it was charming.

"Thanks. I'm glad I'm good for something," she said. "I always helped my mom cook, but I never had time to learn."

"No problem. We've got this," Alex said as he headed out to the patio and lit the barbecue. "You can help with the corn."

"What—what do I do?" she called after him.

"Shuck the corn," he called back.

"That I can do," she said, and by the time the coals were lit and he went back into the house, she was halfway done.

"So we grill these?" she asked.

"Yes, and then you add the secret sauce."

"And what is that?"

"Watch and learn," he said with a laugh. He mixed mayonnaise, Mexican cheese, cilantro and spices together and set it in the refrigerator.

"Mayo? On corn? If I'd known that's what it was I might not have eaten it."

"Ah, but you know how magic it is, right? Nothing like it."

She nodded in agreement, and they carried everything out to the patio. Alex paused for a moment, inhaling deeply of the crisp, salty air and watched as Cassie went out to the cliff and stretched, her hair flowing in the breeze. He couldn't remember a time when he'd been so content, so calm.

"We ran into a blip," Taylor said as she poked her head out the door. "We'll be a little longer, and then I'm on margaritas."

Alex nodded, and said, "We can barbecue all this and it'll be ready when they're done. The sun will be down soon, so I hope they'll make it with the lights in time."

"They will. It may be Baja time, but they'll make it," Cassie said, and for the first time Alex knew exactly what she meant.

As they cooked, several people who'd helped them over the past few days came by and Alex was happy to serve them a plate of the delicious meat, and beans, rice and tortillas to go with it. Every single person raved about the corn, and he knew his grandmother would be proud.

It was a lively group, and Alex had had more fun than he had in years doing this project. Raul popped his head out the door and said, "I think we're ready."

A hush fell over the group of friends and neighbors and Alex reached for Cassie's hand. Applause and whistles erupted as the lights strung along the pillars lit the patio.

"You did it," Cassie said as she rushed to hug Raul and Taylor as they came around, their faces beaming.

"We all did it," Raul said, shaking Alex's hand and patting him on the back.

The visitors slowly dwindled. The four friends rested and ate, and as the sun set and dusk fell over the sea, Cassie said, "I can't believe we all pulled this off. My mother will be thrilled, and I'm pretty impressed with us."

They laughed and toasted to each other. Alex looked from the house to the sea, and up the beach to where the dunes rose—which would soon be tennis courts, with lights that would blot out the stars. He crossed over to the cliff, getting in one last look at the ocean before the darkness fell.

He felt Cassie's hand on his shoulder. "What is it, Alex?"

He knew he should tell her, but he just couldn't. She was beautiful, charming—and he knew if he told her, she'd likely never speak to him. He was the enemy, and he wanted this to last a while longer, no matter how selfish.

"Just enjoying the beauty I see all around me, Cassie."

She nodded. "It's overwhelming, isn't it," she said innocently.

"Yes. Yes, it is."

They returned to the house, lights fully ablaze.

"Wow, we've never had this much light. Ever," Taylor said.

"Well done, you two. Cassie and I may have wielded hammers with minimal injury, but you two put this together. I could never have figured that out."

"Speaking of that, I'd love to take us all out to dinner tomorrow night. Taylor and I need to clean up around here, but dinner at the Rancho tomorrow? On me? I can't thank you all enough, but I can do that."

Alex and Raul both bowed slightly in her direction. "We have some work to catch up on, but tomorrow evening would be lovely. Thank you," Alex said. "Want us to stay and help with the dishes?"

Cassie laughed. "I can't cook, I can't do calculations, but I can do dishes," she said as she pushed them both toward the door. "Thank you for everything, and we'll see you tomorrow night."

TEN

The next afternoon, Cassie took every item of clothing she'd brought for the trip, glanced at it and threw it on the bed.

"I've got to find something decent to wear," Cassie said, eyeing herself in the mirror. "He's only seen me in work mode, or when I looked like a drowned rat. Hoping to do better than that for tonight."

"I don't know why. I normally pack like I'm camping, but I threw a couple of extra things in knowing your head wasn't exactly screwed on right at the time for packing."

She was right. When Cassie had found out about the demise of the vaquita sanctuary and made plans to head down south, all she'd considered was what she'd be wearing to the news conference. The rest was an afterthought.

"Let's pick the best one. You need to look your best tonight, my friend."

Cassie looked at her friend in the mirror and frowned. "It's just a thank-you dinner. Nothing special."

"Right. I see how you two look at each other like nothing's special. Sure."

"Okay, so I like him. A lot," Cassie said as she flipped through the dresses Taylor had brought. She actually liked Alex more than a lot, but she wasn't ready to say it out loud. They barely knew each other. She hadn't even told him about the vaquita. "And what about you and Raul?"

Taylor shook her head. "He's very nice and funny and obviously brilliant. But we're math buddies. That was one of the most fun projects I've ever done, but no spark. Which is fine. Fun to have a friend that's a guy. And a smart guy at that."

Cassie nodded with understanding. She turned her attention to the subject of her attire, and borrowed a white dress that drifted over her legs and wouldn't rub her sting, which was still a little tender. Swiping some gloss over her lips, she caught herself in the mirror. Not too bad, she thought.

"That's a lot of dressing up for you, Cass." Taylor threw a pair of pink sandals at her friend. "Finishing touch."

They arrived at Rancho Del Sol right on time, and Alex was outside the restaurant waiting for them. Both girls let out a little gasp when they spotted him, outside under the palapa dressed in a cotton shirt and khaki pants. He was every bit the handsome Latin gentleman, down to the embroidery on his shirt.

"Wow, he's easy on the eyes," Taylor said, with a wink to her friend. "You're going to have fun tonight, I hope."

"What do you mean me? You and Raul are eating with us."

Taylor stayed in the driver's seat as Alex came around to open the door for Cassie, but winked at her friend. "No, I'm meeting him over by the palapas in the bar on the beach, so I'll just drive down there. I don't think I'll be here long. Can you get her home?" she asked, Alex within earshot.

"Of course," he said, nodding at Taylor while holding his hand out for Cassie. His eyes widened in surprise as he saw her. "You look lovely."

Cassie smiled and tried not to wince as she eased her tired leg out of the Jeep. She wasn't successful, and Alex's arm shot behind her waist to help her. She felt comfortable, almost familiar with him and was grateful to him for looking out for her. He helped her over to the door, and she turned and waved at Taylor as she drove off toward the beach bar.

"Looks as if you're still a little unsteady. Does it hurt much anymore?" he asked as he held her arm and pulled out her chair. She sat down and gaped at the beautiful view out the tall glass windows from the best table in the restaurant, one she knew was for reservations only.

"Only when I get tired," Cassie said with a wry smile. "Gets better all the time, though. I really appreciate you looking after me."

"I couldn't take my eyes off of you from the moment I saw you, so it was easy," he said with a comfortable grin.

"Is this something you do frequently?"

"Have dinner with beautiful women?" His eyes darkened, and he looked away. "I do not have time for such things, and should probably not be doing it now."

Cassie wanted to know more about why such a handsome and skilled man wouldn't, but his frown discouraged further questions along those lines. She wanted to change his mood, and said, "No, saving people from drowning is what I meant. And helping them get the lights back on."

He started, as if coming back to the present. "Oh, I misunderstood. No, I don't do that much either."

"It's not something that happens much for you in the Navy?"

He gazed at his plate, picking up his fork, absently moving it from one side of his plate to the other. "I am no longer in the Navy. It was a brief period for me, something required before I entered the family business."

He grew quiet, and the twinge in her belly told Cassie she should step back. She hoped there would be time for her to delve deeper into this subject later, but for now, she kept it light, grateful when the waiter came and let them know what the specials of the evening were.

"So, when was the last time you had the famous Sea of Cortez blue shrimp?"

Alex smiled, seeming relieved at the change of subject. "Ah, my favorite. May I order for us both?" he asked, checking first to make sure she wasn't allergic to any particular foods, and to gauge her heat tolerance. Food in Mexico could be very hot, with jalapeno peppers almost a revered national vegetable.

"I can handle it as hot as they can make it," she laughed, and she knew she had made the right decision when she was greeted again with his warm, wide smile.

They worked their way through shrimp cocktail, Mexican style, with avocados, tomatoes, jalapenos and lime and moved on to locally caught fish with tortillas, rice and beans.

She refrained as best she could from prying questions about his background, but Alex wanted to know all about Cassie's experiences here in the Baja. They'd already spent hours in the past few days talking about their mutual love of sand and sea, but she'd purposefully avoided talking about the vaquita. She looked out at the crashing waves and thought it was time he should know. She felt a twinge of regret that she hadn't told him already about something so near and dear to her heart—to her life.

"We've talked a lot about things around Baja, but I haven't mentioned my favorite. The vaquita."

Alex frowned and leaned back in his chair. "You mean the little dolphin that live around here?"

Exasperated—although she shouldn't be as it happened almost every time—Cassie said, "Not dolphin. They're porpoises. Not the same thing."

Alex smiled and said, "That's a difference probably only a marine biologist would know. I'm not that."

She smiled and reached up to her necklace. "Well, I am. It's Dr. Cassie Lewis, marine biologist, and the vaquita have been my research project for almost five years. It's my aim to save them."

Alex actually gulped loud enough for Cassie to hear it, and she stopped, puzzled. "Are you all right?"

"Yes, yes, I'm fine," he said, wiping his forehead with a napkin. "Please, continue."

Words tumbled out. Her enthusiasm got the better of her as it always did. Involved in her story, Cassie didn't notice as the napkin Alex was holding turned into smaller and smaller pieces on the table. He grew quiet as she touched on her concern for the vaquita and their imminent extinction. Somewhere during the evening, he reached for her hand with compassion as she gave a heartfelt description of the ravages of the fishing nets and seeing their carnage on the beach.

"Your concern for the vaquita is quite touching." Alex sat back in his chair and piled the napkin shreds. "Have you considered how it is necessary that Mexican people must earn a living? The desert is harsh and fishing is the only way to feed their families."

Cassie's eyes flashed as she leaned forward, her cheeks flushed. "Feeding a family, and keeping only that, or selling what you can in a small store is entirely different from large-scale commercial fishing, Alex. With the gill nets, they scoop for everything and anything in their path, and toss back the species that are not big sellers. Vaquita, sea turtles, all kinds of things. It's the gill nets that are the problem— the vaquita get caught too and can't untangle them- selves. They can't surface for air and they drown. We found dead ones washed up on the shore decades ago, and it's only gotten worse. These are not people feeding their families who are killing the vaquita."

She leaned forward, hoping her tears wouldn't scare him off. "Let me show you what I'm talking about. Come out on a panga with me tomorrow. I have an extra day before I meet with the developers."

He stared at her for a moment, his face blank but his eyes cloudy. It was as if he was trying to decide something, and she hoped he'd decide to come with her.

He nodded slowly. "I have everything ready for work the day after. I would love to see the water through your beautiful eyes," he said, reaching for her hand.

She lowered her eyes, an odd sensation enveloping her. She felt almost shy, something she wasn't accustomed to feeling, about sharing her vaquita with him. It wasn't something she often did, as she was so protective of them. "Great. Meet me on the beach at nine a.m. I'll pack a lunch."

"I've been jabbering forever about all this, Alex." The bottle of wine they shared had long been empty, and their coffee was now cold. "Tell me why you're here. You mentioned work. I thought you were here for vacation."

Alex looked down into his coffee. He picked up his spoon, stirred his coffee and looked up at her, his eyes blank. "It's very complicated, Cassie. I am here to work, to do a job for my family company. It's not one I'm happy about doing."

Cassie had been looking out the window toward the sea. She gasped, and he turned to see what had gotten her attention. The moon, orange and shimmering, rose majestically from the water. He grabbed her hand, easing her out of her chair and they laughed as they walked out into the cool air toward the beach. His arm slipped around her waist, spreading warmth with his touch. She still hobbled, and her thigh throbbed with every step, but he helped guide her down to the water, helping her sit on the sand.

"I never get used to this sight. It's breathtaking," Cassie said, as the round moon beamed down. She took off her shoes and wriggled her toes, relishing the luscious feeling of the warm sand. She reached for her hair as it blew in the breeze, and his hand met hers as she pulled it to the nape of her neck. Alex sat down beside her, throwing his shoes behind them as well.

"I love how the reflection of the full moon looks like a walkway, right up to it. When I was a little girl, I thought I could walk all the way up and then I would be able to see everything. All the vaquita, all the Baja. Then I could make things right."

He turned toward her and took her hand. "Cassie, there are things you need to know about me. More than I've told you."

"I think I know everything I need to know," she said as she drank in the beautiful evening. The glow of the moon in his amber eyes almost made her feel woozy. Her breath came more quickly, and she reached up to touch the waves of his hair. He was kind, thoughtful, handsome, funny and smart. What more could she need to know?

Alex reached for her wrist, and pulled her hand to his lips, his pained expression confusing to her. Kissing her palm, he leaned toward her. Her screech pierced the night as his hand came to rest on her thigh. He jumped up in horror as she doubled over, the pain shooting through her leg like lightning. She tried to catch her breath, and all she could see was the stars swirling inside her head.

"I'm so sorry. I'm so sorry, I forgot." He rammed his hands into the pockets of his khakis. "I hurt you."

"Yes, thank you. I'm okay. It was just an accident," Cassie said.

Cassie laid back and looked up at the stars, catching her breath as the internal flashes of light subsided. As the pain left her, she suddenly heard her own laughter peeling through the night. Here she was with the most handsome, interesting man she'd met in a long while, and she couldn't even do anything about it. This must be some kind of cosmic joke, she thought.

Alex stopped pacing and sat back down beside her. Her laughter rippling through the night had captured him as well, and they both laughed together at the absurdity of it all.

"I'd better take you home, Senorita. I don't think you can handle much more of this." His voice was serious, but the twinkle in his eye made Cassie braver than she might otherwise have been.

"Thank you, kind sir. I think it may be all I'm up to. Could you help me up?"

Without hesitation, Alex swooped down, picking Cassie up and turning toward the restaurant, avoiding the bandage on her thigh. "I can do better than that."

Cassie noticed all eyes on her as they passed the restaurant toward the car. It was like a bad movie. With that fleeting thought, though, she realized that now, this moment, she felt the most peaceful she had in a very long time. She sank into his embrace and allowed him to get her safely home.

ELEVEN

"You're up early," Raul said as he shuffled onto the patio, a cup of coffee in his hands.

"Yes," Alex replied, not sure even where to begin. He'd come home from dropping Cassie off and confirmed his worst suspicions. He'd dug the report about the vaquita sanctuary out of his briefcase and stared at the cover, and the name of the author, for what had felt like a lifetime. Then he'd read it, cover to cover. Her passion and commitment came through on every page and not only was she brilliant, she was determined. And he and his family were the ones standing in her way. His heart ached. He shook his head and filled in his friend.

"You mean she's THE Dr. Lewis, the one who wrote the whole report?" his friend asked at the end of his story, even though he'd confirmed it at the beginning. It definitely was a lot to take in.

"Yes," Alex mumbled. "And now I'm really in a bind. I'm going out on a panga with her today to spy for vaquita."

Raul whistled slowly. "Wow. I can't believe she'd take you, knowing who you are."

Alex cleared his throat and rubbed the back of his neck. He set the report down on the table between them and sighed.

"Are you telling me she doesn't know? You didn't tell her?" Raul asked, his eyes wide.

Alex stood and walked to the edge of the patio, looking out over the water. "I couldn't do it. If I told her, she'd hate me and never speak to me again. I didn't —I don't—want that."

"Alex—"

Alex held up his hands to stop his friend. He knew what he would say. And he agreed.

"I know. I'll tell her. I'll tell her today."

Raul poured himself another cup of coffee and took a long sip. "Hopefully she won't throw you off the boat."

Alex laughed, but it felt hollow. She had every right to throw him off the boat and more. He had known exactly how they all felt about the resort, almost from day one. And he hadn't told her. It felt like downright lying.

"I have a phone call in to my mother. Maybe I can salvage this. Maybe she'll agree to the sanctuary, and Cassie might forgive me."

Raul joined his friend and looked at the view. "Even if she got the sanctuary, you're going to be pretty unpopular with everybody around here. They all hate the idea of the resort. It's not just the sanctuary."

Alex leaned forward, his palms on the short wall surrounding the patio. "It's not just me. They're going to hate you, too. You haven't told Taylor, either."

Raul plopped down on the chaise lounge, wiping away purple bougainvillea leaves. "No, I haven't, and I feel like a jerk, too. I get it. But at least we're just friends. We have nothing going on like you and Cassie."

"What do you mean?"

Raul laughed. "Taylor and I are just friends. But it's obvious you guys have feelings for each other. Taylor mentioned it, too."

Alex knew he was right. It was obvious to Alex, as well, and he'd been up most of the night trying to think of ways to salvage the situation. He just hadn't come up with any.

He glanced at his watch. "I've got to go. I'm supposed to meet Cassie at nine. I don't want to be late."

Raul clapped his hand on his friend's shoulder. "I think you've got bigger problems than being late, but good luck."

TWELVE

Taylor was asleep when Alex dropped Cassie off, and walked her to the door. Cassie was so embarrassed about how the evening had ended that she hurried inside after confirming their arrangements for the next day. After she took the bath Alex had insisted she take to help her leg, she turned off the light that Taylor had left on for her, and sat for a moment on the patio watching the moon trail ever higher in the sky, its light still sparkling on the water.

She'd been disappointed that she hadn't had even more time with Alex, but she was looking forward to taking him out on the water the following day and just had a feeling he'd understand more about the vaquita, about Baja and about her after he'd seen it through her eyes.

She fell into bed, thinking she was exhausted, but

she didn't sleep well. Thoughts of how disappointed she was at the end of her evening with Alex intruded in the darkness. She remembered his interrupted kiss, her pain—none of it had contributed to the night she'd thought they might have. She laughed as she limped to the refrigerator to make a picnic lunch for what she hoped would be a better chance for them to get to know each other.

She watched the small boats leaving for their day of fishing as she packed her ice chest with chips, sandwiches, water, sodas and a couple of bottles of beer. The sheer number of small fishing boats—panga—made her nauseous with the thought of how many vaquita might be caught in the nets meant for commercial fish. The Mexican government had its protective laws, sure, but there wasn't much monitoring here in the northern Baja waters. It was rare to spot an official vessel of any kind, and most fishermen, local or not, didn't even bother with the required fishing license.

As she packed the last sandwich, Taylor shuffled into the kitchen, rubbing her eyes.

"Did you have fun?" she asked, as Taylor leaned up against the kitchen counter and poured herself a cup of coffee, both hands wrapped around it as she inhaled deeply.

"Amazing," was all Taylor could get out, her hands gripping her mug as she stared off into space.

Cassie shook her head as her friend had trouble forming words. Taylor always had a guy around of some kind, but Cassie had never seen her like this. "Earth to Taylor. Details, girlfriend. Anything has to be better than my story of last night."

Taylor snapped back to the present with a sheepish smile. "I certainly didn't think any of this would happen," she said, taking small sips of her hot coffee. "Raul is a genius when it comes to spreadsheets. We came back here, and he helped me solve a math and pivot table problem I've been struggling with for weeks."

Cassie stared at her friend for a moment before laughing. That wasn't at all what she'd expected to hear. But glancing at Taylor's t-shirt that read, "A day without math is...just kidding. I have no idea," should have reminded her what her friend found fascinating.

"Sounds like a magical evening," Cassie said with a laugh.

"Very funny. It was fun and nothing you say can ruin it. We're just friends—friends who love math." Taylor said, her eyes bright. "You look like you're on your way out. What's up?"

Cassie reached for the box of salsa she'd made and set it in the ice chest, closing the lid. "We're going out on a panga this morning to see if we can find any vaquita. He's curious about them, and I'm hoping we get to see some today."

"Oh, I'm shocked. What else would you be doing?" Taylor had been listening to Cassie talk about the vaquita for more years than she could count. "For you, vaquita. For me, graphs."

Cassie laughed as she told her friend about her night, and how it had ended. "I'm hoping for better opportunity today," she said, pulling her cotton cover-up over her. "Want to come along?"

Taylor shook her head. "Been there, done that. No offense."

Cassie rolled her eyes. "None taken."

"Besides, don't you want to spend some time alone with Alex? Sounds like you like him, and you'd have more fun alone."

"Well, alone with Diego," Cassie said as she carried the ice chest out to the Jeep.

"Ah, Diego. There's that. But he's part of the family. You'll have a great time."

A black blur tore down the driveway, almost knocking Cassie off her feet.

"Whiskers, stop," Taylor yelled, chasing the mutt toward the water.

"Hey," Jimmy said as he shuffled toward the front door. "How you feeling?"

Cassie looked down at the bandage she'd fastened around her thigh, just to keep it clean. "Better. Much better, although last night was rough. Yesterday I ran into the corner of a table and—well—it all hurt again."

"No infection, though?" he asked, cocking his head. "No red or oozing?"

"Gross," Taylor said as she walked back toward the Jeep, whiskers at her heels.

Cassie laughed and stepped back as Jimmy put the ice chest in the back of the Jeep. "Thanks. And no, no red or oozing."

"Good thing you weren't a doctor, Taylor," Jimmy said as he tipped his hat and whistled for Whiskers to follow him, heading down the dirt road to his house.

"Yes, it is a good thing," Taylor called behind him. "And it's a good thing that graph paper doesn't bleed."

Cassie eased herself behind the wheel and pulled out the keys. "Guess we both landed in the right spots."

"Yep, and now you can go and marvel all day at the vaquita."

Scrunching her nose, Cassie said, "You care as much as I do that the vaquita don't disappear. I just won't tell anybody."

Taylor nodded solemnly as Cassie turned the engine over. "No, please don't tell anybody. I get teased enough about math as it is."

Cassie waved as she pulled out onto the short road down to the beach, going along the several houses in between their house and the arroyo. They were all so different—some made of the beautiful fire brick, some plywood, some just trailers with shade covers over them. But they were all beautiful in their own way, covered with brightly colored Mexican tile ceramics in the shapes of the sun, the moon, birds and even lizards. It was quite an unusual place, and she could imagine how Alex would think it was—different. It was like she was seeing it for the first time again, through his eyes. And she looked forward to showing him the most important part of her world through hers.

THIRTEEN

Cassie arrived at the beach to find the panga waiting for them. Cassie had contacted Diego as soon as she'd gotten up. He was her favorite guide and one she had been out on the water with countless times. They had met when she was little, and while he'd taken them all out on fishing expeditions in times past, he had been patiently taking her out on her research trips for the past few years. He had become a true friend of the family, as Taylor pointed out.

"Cassie, it's so good to see you. You are as lovely as ever," Diego said as he kissed her hand with a little bow.

"Oh, Diego, it's so good to see you," she said, pulling him closer for a good, big hug. He dropped his eyes, and she remembered she was in Mexico, a culture with very different customs. Hugs between men and women weren't common. She frequently forgot, though, and she hoped Diego was a bit used to her ways.

"Are we looking for vaquita again today, little one?" His lilting accent always made her feel safe and comfortable.

"Yep, as usual. It's not a research trip, though. Just a fun one, so you're off the hook. Not the usual excitement." She opened the back of the jeep and lifted out her supplies.

Diego laughed, throwing a glance over his shoulder at Cassie. "There hasn't been one dull trip, Cassie. I know how you are."

She pulled her sleeves back and slathered herself with sunscreen. "I have a guest today, Diego, so we have to be on our best behavior. Hoping to see a pod or two. Have you seen many lately?"

He shook his head slowly as he placed the ice chest in the bow of the panga. His feet in the water, he turned to her, head lowered. "They are almost gone. Many are caught in the gill nets and are just thrown overboard, left for dead. They wash up on the shore. We see more every day."

"What's happened?" Diego asked, moving quickly to Cassie. "That's a pretty big bandage."

"Oh, I got hit by a sting-ray. The pain was awful, and I panicked. A man on the beach saved me from drowning. He's our guest today."

"Thank God for him. We'll be careful today," he said as he moved back toward the panga.

They both turned toward the road as Alex arrived on his four-wheeler.

"Good morning, Alex. I'm glad you're here," Cassie said as Alex jumped off the quad and walked toward the panga, his long legs making quick work of it. He took her hand, his warm lips resting lightly on her hand, his eyes not leaving hers for one second. She looked down, feeling the heat rise in her cheeks and her stomach tighten. "Alex, this is Diego, our guide for the day," Cassie said as he walked over to the panga.

Alex walked over to Diego, his bright smile disarming the shy fisherman. Holding out his hand, he said, "It's a pleasure to meet you, Senor."

Diego was a friendly man, and Cassie was confused at his hesitation. His eyes rested on Alex's face, and he seemed frozen, not moving at all.

"Diego?" Cassie said, walking to him and putting her hand on his arm. "Are you all right?"

Shaking his head slowly, he looked up and smiled at Alex, extending his hand. "I'm fine. It's very nice to meet you, Alex. Mucho gusto." They shook hands and busily loaded the remaining gear in the panga, ready for their adventure.

Alex helped push the boat away from the shore at Diego's direction and hopped in when it was free of the sand. They settled in for the ride, and as the engine hummed and they pulled away from the shore, Cassie leaned back against the side of the boat and closed her eyes.

Out on the water was where Cassie felt most free. The wind in her hair and the rhythmic bouncing of the panga on the waves always lulled her into a trance. Diego's expert driving allowed her to just relax until they got to the island they were looking for, the Isla Los Lobos, Island of the Wolves, and she stretched out on the long boat for the ride.

Alex grabbed the binoculars and turned his sights to the shoreline. He looked north and south as they traveled toward the island, and asked question after question about the houses dotting the shoreline.

"What campo is that one?" he asked. Cassie gave as detailed descriptions as she knew of the campos and the people who lived there.

"Playa Bonita. The owner decided it was a good idea to charge each resident ten dollars to get in and out of camp. Not a really good business decision," she said, glancing at Diego.

"All the residents abandoned their houses and moved to other campos. Now he's got a camp full of houses and nobody to live there," Diego added. His index finger circled around his ear. "He was loco."

Alex let out a laugh. Lowering the binoculars, he said, "This is a very strange region. I don't understand it, I don't think."

"Well, all the campos technically belong to Mexican citizens, and they run them, kind of like land-lords. So they're all just like little neighborhoods. Our campo is Playa Luna, the one to the north is Campo Saguaro—like that. Like neighborhoods."

"Ah," Alex said as he scanned the shore with the binoculars once again.

Diego slowed the engine and pointed south. Cassie and Alex turned and saw the island, their stop for the day. Its secluded beaches and little white hills glimmered in the morning sun.

Diego pulled into the first cove and looked for a good place to land. Spotting one a bit north, he slowly guided the panga closer to the sand.

Cassie pulled off her cover-up and gingerly put her injured leg over the side of the boat. "Want to swim in?"

"Are you sure you can?" Alex's eyebrows shot up as he quickly took off his shirt.

"Race you," she said, as she pushed off with her good leg, expertly diving to the side of the boat. Alex was fast behind her, splashing into the water and kicking toward shore.

Cassie felt her leg pull as she slowly swam toward shore, her arms doing most of the work. Alex pointed downward to a group of beautiful yellow fish darting back and forth over the sand and between the small rocks. Close enough to shore to stand, she stayed crouched in the shallow water, crabs moving away from her in quick, jagged movements.

"Look what I found," she heard Alex say. Holding up a sunflower starfish, he laughed, twisting it over and over in his hand. "I've never seen a purple starfish with eighteen legs." He studied it for a while, then placed it gently back on the sea floor.

"They're amazing, aren't they? I bet most humans don't even know they exist, and they are all over out here," she said, holding out a sand dollar to him. A wave crashed by at that moment, and she was knocked into him, her hands grabbing his waist to steady herself.

"I like the waves, too. I like all of it," he said, smiling down at her.

By the time they arrived on the beach, Diego had the ice chest and blankets out of the panga and had set up a makeshift picnic area. The bright umbrellas couldn't be missed against the white sand and blue sea.

"Cerveza?" Diego asked Alex, holding out a cold beer from the ice chest.

Alex took it, holding the wet bottle up to his forehead to cool off. "Gracias. Do you have an opener?"

Cassie and Diego both looked quickly at each other, smiles spreading. "You don't need an opener. You have her," Diego said, nodding his head at Cassie.

What the heck, Cassie thought. He may as well get to know the real me.

She reached in her bag and took out her pocketknife. Opening it quickly, she held her hand tightly around the bottle, bracing the flat end of the knife under between the bottle cap and her finger and popped off the cap of the beer bottle, sending it flying directly into the ice chest.

Alex's mouth dropped open as he took the bottle from Cassie's extended hand. "Where did you learn to do that?"

"It's something I learned here in Baja. My dad always said it's the best thing I ever learned, and I didn't need a Master's Degree for it. He taught me before he died." She smiled, opening another beer for herself and one for Diego. "It's something I'm particularly proud of. I can also whistle really loud with my fingers. My dad taught me that, too."

Alex laughed, shaking his head at the sight. "I'm sorry you lost your father. I imagine I would have liked him. And I don't know any women who can open a bottle that way."

"Well, you just haven't met many Baja women," Cassie said, handing sandwiches to both men. "Let's eat, so we can look for some vaquita."

Cassie packed the trash and remaining supplies as they finished lunch. As Diego set about taking down the umbrellas and finishing the packing, Cassie and Alex walked toward the shoreline.

"So, tell me what we're looking for and where we're looking," Alex said.

FOURTEEN

Back on the water, Cassie turned her trained eye to the horizon. She knew the vaquita were very elusive and with fewer than a hundred left, the odds of spotting any were low. The smallest of all porpoise species, adults were only five feet long, and they didn't travel in large pods like common dolphin. It was rare to see more than two or three together at a time, so you had to be a patient spotter to see them at all.

They circled the island slowly, as she had had her best luck around this area in spotting and categorizing her vaquita. "I didn't bring all of my equipment from the Institute this trip, Diego. I didn't think I'd be on the water with you this time," Cassie said.

"I don't think it will matter, Cassie. We've spotted vaquita every time we've been out together. Almost a miracle. I rarely see them on other trips," Diego said, steering into another cove on the opposite side of the island.

"What's that on the beach?" Alex asked, turning his binoculars to the approaching white sand. "It looks like something big."

Cassie turned her binoculars the direction he was pointing. As they got closer, her pulse quickened and her hands started to sweat. "Oh, no. It can't be," she said, her knuckles whitening as her grip on the binoculars tightened. Her eyes stung with tears, and she lowered the binoculars, looking away.

Alex's slowly lowered his binoculars and looked at Diego. Diego's eyes were wet, too, and he increased their speed, moving faster toward the beach.

Cassie took a deep breath and pulled her hair back into a ponytail. The back of her hands brushed the tears from her cheeks, and she pulled on her shoes. She was back to business, now.

As the panga's bow met the sand, she was out of the boat in a flash, ignoring the pain in her thigh. She strode quickly over to the object, sitting down hard in the sand next to the beautiful sea creature.

Jumping out of the boat and hurrying behind Cassie, Alex stood for a moment, silent, curious at the sight before him. The porpoise lay still, its white under-belly not moving. His short snout and black rings around his eyes were something he hadn't seen before.

Cassie stared at the still creature, tears streaming

down her cheeks. She reached out a hand, resting it lightly on its side. She stroked its skin lightly, looking as Diego arrived.

"It's just a baby," Diego said, moving closer and kneeling down beside the animal.

"Exactly what we can't afford to lose," Cassie said, her fist clenching as she stroked the vaquita with her other hand. "I'd say it's only about five months old, this one. Darn nets."

Alex reached out slowly to touch the vaquita, his eyes clouding as he stroked its lifeless flesh. He cleared his throat and pulled his hand back, staring at the fascinating markings.

The sea was quiet in this cove, the waves only ripples on the beach. Alex started to speak, but Cassie quickly said, "Sh," her attention drawn to the back of the panga. "Do you hear them?" she said, her eyes growing sad again.

The clicks grew louder as bigger ripples formed in the still water behind the panga. Suddenly, two fins emerged from the calmness of the sea. "Be still." Cassie stood slowly, backing way from the baby vaquita, motioning for Alex and Diego to come, too.

As the three backed away and sat down against a rock across the cove, the two porpoises drew closer to the shore. The dead young porpoise rocked back and forth with the ripples, half in and half out of the water. The two adult vaquita inched forward and Cassie felt her throat catch, the tears come. Alex and Diego stared at the scene before them, their eyes clouding under furrowed brows.

Cassie felt Alex take her hand, stroking her forearm. She laid her head on his shoulder, trying her best not to sob, as the adult vaquita swam back and forth along the shore, as close to their calf as they could get without beaching themselves. Their clicks became quick and urgent as they swam faster, back and forth.

As if suddenly in agreement, the porpoises stopped for a moment, becoming silent in the still waters in front of their offspring. Slowly, they circled around each other as if in the perfect demonstration of the yin and yang symbol, and then they were gone.

Cassie felt as if all the air had been taken out of the sky as she gulped back her tears. She felt Alex's hand stroke her head, brushing her hair off her forehead, and brushing away her tears. His grasp tightened around her, and she let herself sob as grief poured through her.

Finally, she stood and walked toward the panga. Alex stood to follow her, but Diego pulled him back.

"Leave her to it. She needs to do this," Diego whispered, although Cassie heard him.

She brought her supplies and quickly took measurements of the vaquita—but hadn't brought her scale to weigh it. She could kick herself for that. She closed her eyes and gently wriggled her hand under its head, grasping its tail with her other hand. She lifted it gently, reverently, guessing at its weight and marking it down in her book.

Next she measured it, looked for any markings and noted them in her book as well. She described its size, its length, its markings—any identifying factors she could see. She took several pictures with her phone, making sure they were time-stamped. Then she wrote about seeing the parents, and tears plopped on her notepad, making the blue ink run.

And when she was done, she packed up her stuff and walked back to the vaquita. She knelt alongside it, stroking its head one last time, telling it she would do everything in her power to save its family.

Alex approached behind her, and as she stood he reached his arm around her.

"Shouldn't we bury it or something?" he asked softly.

She shook her head and looked up at the sky, her hand over her eyes.

"No. She needs to go back to the sea. Other things need her to survive. It's part of the cycle of life, even though it's hard to watch sometimes. Everything's got an enemy."

Alex nodded. "And these porpoises seem to have more enemies than most."

She looked up at him. "Yes, they do. In addition to regular predators and gill nets, they have the resort. The resort is their biggest threat, now that they won't allow the sanctuary. We can't stop the fishermen, but we had a chance to build a safe place for the vaquita to breed, to get strong again. Now, I'm not sure there's anything I can do. And who will protect them if not us?"

FIFTEEN

On the return trip, Cassie's emotions were raw and closer to the surface than she wanted them to be. Back on the shimmering water, she had stretched out in the panga, drinking in the smells and sounds, trying to push away the memory of what they had seen. Alex hadn't spoken since they'd left the cove, and Diego was like a statue on his perch by the engine.

As Cassie basked in the warm sun, she felt Alex lean back beside her. Her arm rested over her face, shielding her eyes against the sun. He gently tugged at her hand, again lifting it to his lips. "I had no idea these vaquita even existed, let alone the threat of extinction." He was so close she could smell his presence, and it calmed her.

"There are only about a hundred left on the entire planet, Alex. Make that ninety-nine. If something isn't done, they'll be gone in less than two years. I just can't let that happen."

He sat up on the bench, his long legs cramped in the small panga. "It's truly a tragedy," she said finally, his intense expression tugging at her heart.

"Yes, it is," he said, reaching over and holding his hand in the cool spray of the panga. He lifted his hand swiftly, drenching her with water. She wasn't ready to laugh yet, but she smiled at his attempt to distract her from her sorrow. They stretched out in the boat and fell silent until they reached the beach.

The panga glided to a stop on the shore, skimming onto the sand. Cassie and Alex slid over the side of the panga, wading through the warm water to the shore. She had wanted to show him a vaquita and hadn't expected to find the scene she did. Her emotions were still on the surface as Alex held his hand out to her for the ice chest, then again to help her out of the panga. She turned to thank Diego and he nodded, his face like stone.

Her breath catching in her throat, she walked beside Alex in silence, remembering their magical vaquita sighting. Happy that they shared such an important experience, she didn't think she could be more content than she was at this moment.

Alex took her hand as they walked back up to the restaurant. "I had no idea about the fishing of the endangered species, Cassie. My time in the Navy was not spent in the Sea of Cortez, and I've spent very little time here on land, either. It's all been on paper to me."

"On paper? You mean like on a map?"

"Well, yes, sort of. I don't know how to explain this to you. There are things about me that you don't know, and I am sure you don't want to know."

Puzzled and hurt, she looked up at him. His amber eyes bore into her, startling her with their intensity. She wanted to know everything about him. All of it. He seemed dejected and hopeless, and Cassie didn't understand why.

Carrying their supplies up to the jeep, Cassie spotted Taylor and Raul under one of the palapas, sipping drinks from huge seashells.

Cassie put her fingers in her mouth and whistled loudly, Taylor's head snapping in her direction, laughing. "I knew that had to be you," Taylor chirped, running over to the jeep. "How was the trip?"

"I'll have to tell you about it later," Cassie said, stealing a glance at Alex. His face was blank, and his eyes were still dull.

"Did you all have a nice time?" Raul asked as he joined them, his smile wide. "Did you have a chance to talk?"

Alex's eyes flickered for a moment as he looked over at Raul. The two men stared at each other for what seemed minutes.

"No," Alex answered harshly.

Confused, she glanced at both men. They'd spent

days together, and this was the first time she'd heard Alex use a harsh tone of any kind. What could be an issue with Raul? "We're going inside to have a drink. Want to come?"

"Fine with me," Taylor said, turning to Raul. "Is that all right with you?"

"I suppose it's fine," he said, looking over to the restaurant. "Briefly."

Taylor and Cassie stole a quick glance at each other. Cassie re-arranged her cover-up and touched her hair. "I think I need to make a stop in the ladies' room. I'll catch up."

Cassie walked toward the restaurant, past the brick arches and under the palapas, pulling open the door of the restaurant and meeting room area. Employees were setting up for tomorrow's ribbon-cutting ceremony and the check-in line for the small rancho was long.

Winding her way through the people, trying to find the restroom, she felt butterflies in her stomach about tomorrow's events. She knew there would be throngs of people and reporters there. She hoped her passion would carry her message, and the resort owners would reconsider.

As she passed by the room where the press conference was to be held, she couldn't help but peek her head inside. On the wall a huge map of the proposed resort, with a golf course, restaurants, pool and bungalows along with the main hotel. Her eyes drifted on the drawing to the water, where she saw plans for tennis courts and a marina. The marina was massive, and her heart sank with the thought of all those boats, all that pollution, all those fishermen.

She turned on her heel and headed back toward the door, steeling herself for tomorrow's battle. As she was about to pass through the door, she noticed a display table holding pamphlets for the ceremony. She stopped and looked both left and right, feeling a little sneaky for picking one up, but she did. They were beautiful, glossy pamphlets that no doubt were very expensive with glowing descriptions of the resort and beckoning buyers.

Flipping a brochure over to look at the back, her breath stopped, and she blinked. She blinked hard again, not believing her eyes. There, at the bottom of the brochure, was the smiling face of Alex Vasquez, CEO of Costa Azul International. Alex. Her Alex.

Her heart in her throat, she gripped the brochure tightly. She'd never been as angry as now, and her blood rushed through her veins. Striding into the restaurant, she saw Taylor at a table with Alex and Raul. Alex stood as she made it to the table, his face freezing as he saw her. "What is it, Cassie? Are you all right?"

For the second time in not many days, Cassie Lewis was utterly speechless. She shoved the brochure in Alex's chest, and, with a little extra push, she turned and got to the jeep as fast as she could.

SIXTEEN

Alex felt as if his heart stopped as the brochure Cassie shoved in his chest fluttered to the floor. The second shove for good measure had him rock back on his heels and was made more painful by the look of fury mixed with pain in her eyes. He stood stock still as she ran for the door, dropping his head into his hands as it slammed behind her.

"What the—" Taylor had stopped to pick up the brochure and stared from it to Alex and back down at it again. She even held it up next to him to be sure. "You? CEO of Costa Azul?"

He looked up at her, the shame he was feeling overwhelming.

"Taylor, I can explain," he said, looking away from her withering glare.

"I bet you can. But you've had—" she pretended to

look down at the watch on her wrist, even though she wasn't wearing one. "Let me see, over a week and countless opportunities to do that and you didn't. You lied to her."

Alex shook his head and looked toward Raul for some back-up. He held up his hands and took a step toward Taylor. "I never lied. I swear, I didn't."

Taylor took a step back, shaking her head slowly. "Same thing. You knew she was here to stop this resort— your resort—and didn't say a word. You're a horrible, dishonorable human," she said. She turned her withering glare toward Raul as Alex rubbed the back of his neck.

"And you. A project manager? And you couldn't have told me which project?" she asked, her voice rising.

Raul started to speak, but he got the same treatment Alex had.

"Save it. Just save it, both if you," she said.

Alex thought she looked like she wanted to spit on their shoes, and he wouldn't have blamed her if she had.

She turned on her heel and followed Cassie out the door.

"That didn't go well," Alex said slowly after Taylor stormed off.

"That's an understatement," Raul said. "I suppose it's safe to assume you didn't have the opportunity to tell her today like you'd planned."

Alex glanced sideways at his friend and wanted to shove his elbow in his ribs. "Obviously not. I was going to tell her at lunch. Both of them."

Raul nodded as they each pulled out a stool at the restaurant bar. "Right. I imagine it wasn't easy. But I have to say I warned you."

Elbows on the bar, Alex lowered his head. "I've never felt like such a jerk in my life, to be honest. I know you warned me. I just couldn't do it. I don't understand why."

"Really? You don't?" Raul laughed and held up two fingers to the bartender who delivered two bottles of cold, Mexican beer. Alex looked up as Raul pushed one in front of him, but it didn't even look appealing. In fact, he felt sick.

"No, I don't," he said as he turned the bottle in circles on the polished wooden bar.

"Well, I do. It's written all over your face, and now that I think about it, it makes all the sense in the world."

Alex looked up at his friend, curious what he could mean. "And?"

Raul took a sip of his beer and turned to Alex, his eyes gleaming and a smile tugging at his lips.

"Remember Melissa?"

Alex closed his eyes for a moment, remembering his college sweetheart. He'd loved her with all his heart---or so he'd thought at the time. She'd left him for someone else and it had taken quite a long time to recover, and he'd never been in love since.

"How could I forget?" Alex asked.

"Well, you had the same look on your face when you were with her as you do with Cassie. Except maybe even more so now, if that's possible."

Alex blinked a few times as he looked at his friend. "What do you mean?"

Raul clapped his friend on the shoulder. "Come on, Alex, don't be so dense. I've been around you guys this whole time except for today. The more you found out about her, the worse it got. And I totally get it. She's great."

"She is great, but I still don't see what you're talking about."

Raul leaned forward on the bar and shook his head. "Come on. You know how passionate she is about all of this dolphin stuff."

"Porpoise," Alex corrected, knowing Cassie would want him to.

"Fine, porpoise. But seriously, when she found out you were the one who was going to ruin it all, it makes sense she'd react the way she did."

"It did cross my mind. Maybe that's why I was dragging my feet."

"I'm sure of it, and honestly I don't blame you. It's tough being in love with someone who's pretty much going to hate your guts. I can see why you weren't in a hurry to make that happen."

Alex started at the word love. It hadn't occurred to him that might have been the reason he was holding off. He'd convinced himself that it didn't matter, that it would be fine. But it wasn't fine, and based on the fact that he hadn't even taken a sip of his beer and still felt sick, he knew Alex was right. He was in love.

SEVENTEEN

The wind whipped through her hair as she sped toward Playa Luna. Tears and sand stinging her eyes, she drove as fast as she could, wanting to blow the memory out of her head of Alex pictured in the brochure for the resort. CEO! The same man she had opened her heart to, poured out her fears and passions.

She thought she had felt his heart, too, and now she realized it was all a joke. Had he known who she was when they met? Had he planned it this way, to take her off her game, make her vulnerable? She knew she could be a formidable opponent, especially when it came to her passion for the vaquita. Maybe he was afraid of her.

Her heart pounded as she pulled up to the house. Jumping out of the jeep, she grabbed her beach chair and made the short trek down to the water. As the waves lapped at her feet, she felt the sobs coming.

Giving in to her senses, she sat down in the sand, her head in her hands.

"What is it, Cassie," she heard behind her. "Is it the vaquita?"

She turned and looked up into Diego's concerned eyes. "I don't even know where to start, Diego."

"At the beginning, Cassie, is the best place."

She poured her heart out to her friend, explaining the sanctuary plans and the denial from the resort company. She told him of her injury, how she had met Alex, and how she found out who he really was.

"I feel like such a complete idiot," she said, wiping hot tears from her cheeks.

Diego was silent for a long while as he picked up handfuls of sand and tossed them toward the waves.

"Not all people have the same heart as you," he said finally, turning toward her. His eyes betrayed his emotion, and he pulled the brim of his hat further down his forehead. "Many people don't understand money is not the most important thing in the world. That is why I came to the Baja, to get away."

Cassie turned toward Diego, her eyes bright with confusion. "I thought you were born here," she said.

"No, I had a job and a very large family business before I came here. They wanted to rule the world and ruin many things. I couldn't do it, and I came here to build things people wanted, and leave only a small legacy of happiness." He smiled sadly, taking his hat off and leaning back into the sand. "It seems it has found me again."

Cassie waited for him to speak again, but he didn't. He raised himself from the sand and walked back toward his home up the beach.

As he grew smaller in the distance, Taylor pulled up on her quad, skidding to a stop and narrowly missing Cassie with a spray of sand.

Hopping off the quad, she lowered herself to the sand next to her friend, resting her hand on Cassie's. "That must have been a shocker," she said, squeezing Cassie's hand and leaning forward, her elbows resting on her knees.

"That doesn't even begin to describe how I'm feeling," Cassie said, her hands clenching into fists. "I bared my soul to him, and I thought he understood about the vaquita." Tears of fury welled up in her eyes, and her heart pounded. "He had plenty of chances to tell me who he was, and he didn't. I'm so furious I could spit," she said, using an old expression of her mother's.

Taylor's hand flew to her mouth as she tried not to laugh. "Well, please don't," she said, unable to completely stifle her laugh.

"I understand it may seem funny to you, but I really was falling for him. I thought he was gentle, and kind, and had the same heart I do," Cassie said, letting out a deep sigh.

"Cassie, I've got to be honest with you. Sometimes

you are so blinded by your passion for these porpoises, you don't see clearly. Not everyone has your vision, your understanding of the bigger view of the Baja." Taylor turned sideways in the sand, grabbing her hand. "Look at me, Cassie."

Cassie turned toward her best friend, tears streaming down her cheeks, their salty warmth on her lips. Taylor's blue eyes filled with concern and shone brightly with tears. "So, he wasn't the man you thought he was. That's all there is to it. You'll find someone who does share your heart, and that's the person you're supposed to be with."

Cassie reached out, hugging her friend tightly. The sobs came now, and she again felt grief overtake her.

Taylor held her firmly, wiping her tears from her cheeks. Cassie's sobs turned to sniffles, and Taylor said, "You're not going to let this guy ruin your plans, are you?"

Cassie turned back to the water, clearing her throat. "No. I have work to do."

"Attagirl," Taylor said as they walked back up to the house.

Cassie was already thinking about the next day, and her presentation. She was so deep in thought that she jumped when her phone rang. Cell service was spotty, so she always let people know she'd be mostly unavailable when she headed south, so it surprised her that somebody was getting through. Warmth spread through her chest and tears pricked her eyes when she saw that the somebody was her mom.

"Hi, Mom," she said with a sniffle. "I'm sorry I haven't been able to call you. I'm in Baja."

The silence at the other end of the phone didn't surprise her.

"Oh, wow, I must have missed the message that you were going," her mom said in her worried and annoyed voice. Although they'd been coming down alone for years and had virtually grown up there, their moms always seemed to worry.

"I really am sorry. There's been so much going on, and the cell service is so bad—"

"I know, sweetheart. I'll get over it. Tell me what's going on."

Cassie's mom, Megan, lived a few hours away in a different part of California, but they talked almost every day, so they skipped right to the subject at hand. Cassie poured her heart out, and felt the tears springing to her eyes again.

"Oh, my gosh. Sweetheart, I'm so sorry. This has to be heartbreaking for you, on both counts. Why didn't he just tell you who he was?"

Cassie plopped down on the couch, her elbows on her knees. "I don't know. I can't quite figure it out. But Taylor and I told him we thought the resort should go up in flames when we first met, and I suppose I wasn't very subtle about the vaquita sanctuary."

"Subtle and vaquita should never be in the same

sentence when referring to you, honey," her mom said, and if she was trying to get a little smile out of Cassie, it worked.

"I know, Mom. I am aware that I can be a little—intense about it."

"You sure can. Maybe he just didn't want to let you down."

Cassie shook her head. "No. He's just a coward, that's all."

"Now, Cassie, if he's the CEO of the resort company, he has a job to do, too. One that's likely just as important to him as yours is to you."

"Whose side are you on?" Cassie asked, annoyed that her mother had always had a knack of making her look at all sides of an issue. "I'm the one who's heartbroken here. Your daughter, remember?"

Her mother laughed and Cassie could picture her holding up her hands. "I know. But you know as well as I do that there are always more than one side to an issue. And more than one way to win. Try to remember that, honey. And it's not over until it's over."

"I love you, Mom," Cassie said quietly. "Thanks. I know what I have to do for the vaquita, but I feel a little better."

"Good. I love you, too, and let me know how it goes as soon as you get a chance. Felicia and I will be rooting for you. You don't mind if I fill her in, do you?"

"No, no, of course not. I don't think there's anything you two don't tell each other, anyway."

They'd been best friends so long that they were almost like sisters, and Cassie was happy that she was like an aunt to her.

Her mother laughed. "True. Just wanted to confirm. And tell Taylor I said hello and to give my love to Kyle."

They ended the call and Taylor wandered back in from the patio.

"How's your mom?"

"Good. She said hello, too, to both you and Kyle. How is your brother anyway?"

"I don't know. You know I don't get to see him much these days. Too bad he gets no time off from his residency. If he was here, he'd have a thing or two to say to Mr. CEO. You know he thinks he's your brother, too." Taylor laughed and plopped on the couch beside Cassie. "Too bad big brother's not around. But I'm here. I'll pop him in the nose if you want me to."

Cassie leaned her head on Taylor's shoulder. "Thanks. But I know what I need to do, Alex or no Alex."

Taylor patted her friend on the knee. "Absolutely. You've got this. I know you do."

EIGHTEEN

Cassie's eyes fluttered as the sunlight began to peek in through her bedroom window. Sitting up in bed, the memory of the night before and the events leading up to her pity party explained the state of her bedroom. Her bag was empty, and her clothes were strewn all over and dishes filled the sink.

"Oh, you're finally awake," Taylor handed Cassie a cup of coffee with so much hazelnut creamer in it, it must have tasted like melted coffee ice cream.

"Thanks. Exactly the way I like it," Cassie said with a weak smile. Not even that could cheer her up at this moment.

"Okay, what are you wearing today, Cass? It's your big day, after all." Taylor reached for her red pants and purple top.

Cassie pulled out her black skirt and a black tank top. "Are you seriously going to wear that?" She had originally intended to wear a beautiful, shimmery beige dress, fit for the vaquita, and shell earrings. She remembered stuffing them under her bed last night, wanting to run back home and forget all about Baja, the vaquita and Alex. Today, black seemed appropriate.

"Black? Seriously? This is important." Taylor put her long brown hair in a ponytail and slipped on her purple sandals. "You've got to be 'up' about this. At least wear some jewelry or something."

"I don't feel 'up' at all," Cassie said, as she slipped on a silver bracelet and earrings. Peering into her jewelry bag, she spotted the silver necklace her mother had given her at graduation. It was a beautiful dolphin, and she slipped it over her head for good luck.

Walking to the window, Cassie looked for her shoes. Finding them in the corner, she slipped them on, feeling as if she was as ready as she ever would be to tackle this event.

"You ready?" Taylor called from the kitchen. "We need to get going."

Grabbing her notes, Cassie glanced at herself in the mirror. The dolphin glimmered at her throat, and she hoped it would take any attention away from her swollen eyes.

As they drove up the beach, Cassie mentally noted where the sanctuary should have begun and the plans for the structure flashed through her mind. All that time, all that work—all that hope would be dashed shortly.

"I just can't believe it," she muttered, and Taylor shot her a quick glance.

"Come on, Cassie. Don't give up. Not yet."

After the short drive up the beach, Cassie and Taylor pushed their way through the throngs of reporters at the entrance to Rancho Del Sol. There were cars and flash bulbs everywhere, making it difficult to pass. "So this is what it feels like to be famous," Taylor joked. "It stinks."

"It's not us they're after, it's him. Ridiculous," said Cassie, her fists clenching. "Hope he's close enough so I can pop him one."

"That'll be a great solution, Cass. 'Woman beats up CEO, film at 11.' I can see it now." Taylor grabbed Cassie's hand and pulled her through the throng at the door, shoving people aside as she went. "If you want a bouncer, let me do it. I don't have as much at stake."

"The extinction of an entire species is a big responsibility," Cassie agreed, nodding.

"Those aren't the stakes I was talking about," said Taylor, giving a giant tug on Cassie's hand, leading them into the meeting room.

They took a seat in the back of the room, Cassie hoping to remain unnoticed for as long as possible. The people who had gotten invitations to the ribbon-cutting ceremony were already inside, sipping champagne and milling about, watching video presentations and checking out the maps and artists' renderings in full color.

"It really is a nice resort, and it looks like we're going to be stuck with it," Taylor said. "I can't wait to play tennis here, as long as they stay far away from Playa Luna."

"You are such a traitor," Cassie hissed, poking her elbow into Taylor's ribs.

Wincing, Taylor elbowed back. "I'm a realist, my friend. I work at an airport, and my carbon footprint alone could probably wipe out entire species. I do what I can, but I also know when the train is on the tracks. I hope the best for you, and I'll do everything I can to help, but this train may be unstoppable. I just don't want you to be disappointed."

The event got underway, and Cassie and Taylor listened to long presentations, in Spanish, about how wonderful the resort would be, and how it would help the economy.

"See, I told you," said Taylor. The minister of tourism for Baja California spoke, all smiles, and there was a lot of gleeful handshaking.

The people on the dais were all dressed in expensive suits, and the lone woman wore a Chanel suit with pearls everywhere. To Cassie, she looked like Audrey Hepburn, with a little Latin flavor. She was beautiful, but Cassie wondered how the woman had navigated the sand in those expensive heels.

As Cassie waited through the speeches, she noticed the woman staring at her intently. She studied her notes, sure it was her nerves acting up again. She willed the butterflies to be still, as the time for her to speak came closer.

She looked up from her notes and caught the woman's eye once more, and her natural instinct was to smile. The woman's brows furrowed, and she quickly looked away.

"What was that about?" Taylor said. "What did you do to her?"

"I have no idea who she is. How would I know?"

Cassie heard her introduction and rose to her feet. Making sure she was steady, she walked to the podium, hundreds of eyes on her, wondering who she was. She realized this opportunity to speak was really just a pity move to make the Institute feel like they had some hope, but she really felt there was none.

NINETEEN

As Cassie described the plight of the vaquita in the northern Sea of Cortez, she swept the audience away to her dream of a vaquita breeding sanctuary. At least, she hoped that's what she was doing.

She shared that in the early 1990s, there had been almost one thousand in this small area of the world where they live. Now, there were fewer than a hundred and over thirty per year were lost to the gill nets of the fishermen, both legally and illegally fishing in these waters.

She explained they were the smallest species of porpoise and lived in the more shallow tide lands, feeding off of smaller fish and squid. She let them know the vaquita lived to be about twenty-one years old and had a calf about once every two years, caring for and feeding those calves until they were about five months old. And she shared her experience of the day before, creating with her words a vivid scene of the dead calf and the mourning dance of the parents.

She felt her heart breaking as she spoke, creating as best she could the world of the vaquita as she saw them. She looked up from her notes and was surprised the room was completely quiet, and several of the ladies held tissues to their eyes. The men were somber, and the reporters in the back were scribbling furiously in their notepads. She spotted Taylor in the back, holding two thumbs up and wearing a silly grin.

"The only hope for these creatures is a sanctuary, to hold some of them in captivity to try to increase their numbers enough for them to have a fighting chance. And the only place to do that is here, at Rancho Costa Azul. I hope you'll reconsider and do your part in keeping an entire species from becoming extinct."

Cassie smiled, hopeful she had made her case. She turned to the CEO of the company—Alex—and looked directly at him. "These tidal waters were promised to the Institute to form a breeding ground to ensure the continuation of this majestic species. On behalf of the Scripps Institute of Oceanography, and for the preservation of the endangered vaquita, we ask once again that you allow us to continue with this project."

The room erupted with applause, photographers' cameras flashing by the hundreds. Cassie backed away from the podium as Alex approached, his pained expression tugging at her heart, against her will.

"Thank you, Miss Lewis, for your description of

the vaquita and the risk of extinction. While I am the CEO of Costa Azul International, we are a family-owned company and governed by the board of directors. We will take this issue to a vote this afternoon, and the board of directors will decide how to proceed. Thank you for your time. Now, we can move on to the ribbon-cutting ceremony—"

"Hang on a minute," Cassie said, moving one step back toward the podium. "That's it? You're going to think about it? I don't want to get a letter in the mail. I think you need to decide now, before it's too late."

Behind Alex, Cassie saw the woman in pearls rise slowly from her chair and move beside him. "Young lady, do you know who I am?"

"No, I don't" Cassie said, watching Alex cast his eyes downward, his sagging.

"I am Senora Nina Vasquez, chairman of the board." The tall, slender woman stood erect, her eyes boring into Cassie's. Not blinking, she said, "We have our ways of dealing with family business, Miss Lewis. We will decide and make you aware of our decision."

Cassie stepped backwards as all the blood rushed out of her face. She felt her hands grow cold, the woman's words hitting her like ice.

Cassie wasn't sure she could see through her tears and was thankful that Taylor grabbed her hand and pulled her through the doors in the back. Just before they left, she turned to see Alex standing on the dais, staring after her. She tore her gaze away and followed Taylor to the Jeep.

"Well, that doesn't sound very promising," Taylor said as they turned onto the beach for the drive home.

"No, it doesn't. Not at all. And for all I know, I will get that letter in the mail. We may as well head home."

"We can't, and you know it. I'm certain they'll let you know today or tomorrow. Nobody—Alex—couldn't be that heartless."

"No? He's heartless, all right. All those days, all that time together even out on the water and he never, ever said a word. I think that is the dictionary definition of heartless, don't you?"

"Raul didn't say anything, either. I guess they're really not who we thought they were."

"That's an understatement," Cassie said as she rested her head back on the seat of the car and closed her eyes, not wanting to see the sanctuary beach as they passed it by.

TWENTY

Alex glanced at the clock in his hotel room. Raul had left earlier to meet with the other architects and he'd been on his own since the press conference. He was expected for dinner with his parents shortly, and he wasn't looking forward to it.

The entire past two days had been a disaster. Alex showered and dressed almost in slow motion. When he was ready for dinner, he sat out on the patio and watched the tide go out, exposing much more beach as the waves retreated. The smell of the sea washed over him and several ospreys circled overhead, one carrying a fish. He marveled at the fact that just a few days prior, he didn't even know what an osprey was, let alone how they lived.

He leaned forward, his elbows on his knees. He hung his head, the full awareness of how this place would change—because of him—striking him full force.

He completely understood his family's desire to build here—it was spectacular, and he'd never been anywhere like it. But seeing it through Cassie's eyes, something felt a little different. These people who had lived or visited here for decades would find that their favorite place had changed forever. And it would be his doing—he'd be the villain.

He slipped his keys into his pocket and headed over to the restaurant and right away spotted his parents in a table by the window.

"Mother. Father," he said as he nodded at both of them. "It's nice to see you here."

"And you," his mother said briskly. She looked uncomfortable, and as she'd been very up front about not wanting to be here, it didn't surprise him. "Have you been enjoying your time?"

She didn't seem to sincerely want to know, but he told her anyway. He didn't think his parents had much they wanted to say, so he just started in. He talked about Cassie, how she'd injured her leg, how they'd fixed the lights at her house, about the beautiful brick-work, everything. And when he got to the part about the vaquita and their trip out on the ocean—well, he held nothing back. He told them how much it meant to him, and how beautiful this land was. How beautiful Cassie was, and how he felt about her.

He finally stopped, and his mother had set her fork down and he hadn't even noticed. She was staring at him, her face blank.

He'd been laughing, animatedly sharing his time with them, and he glanced at his father, who was watching his mother with concern.

"Mother, are you all right?"

She cleared her throat and dabbed at the corners of her mouth with her napkin, although he hadn't noticed her eat anything.

"Yes, I'm fine. And if you're going to ask about the vaquita sanctuary, you can hold your breath. That beach is off limits, and if they need to find another one, so be it."

"Mother, it's no detriment to us to donate. In fact, Raul says it would be a great marketing angle, that we're helping the environment and the vaquita."

He sat taller as his mother gave him a withering stare and stood slowly. "I don't care what Raul says, and I won't have you question my judgment. My decision is final."

Alex held his breath as she threw her napkin on the table and stalked out toward the casitas. He and his father both stared after her for a while, and Alex finally turned to him with a million questions. His father shook his head slowly before saying, "Well, I guess that's final."

"Father, I don't understand," Alex said. "I've never known Mother to behave so irrationally. This doesn't make sense. It's a beach, a plot of land, some water. And it means very much to someone I care about. Why would she object?"

His father ran his hand through his silver hair and leaned back in his chair. "You might want to order some dessert. This story might take a while to tell."

Alex did just that, and settled in as his father began to tell him what had happened in their family so many years ago.

When he'd finished, Alex had torn up another entire napkin and his heart ached.

"So you see why she won't change her mind?"

"I do, but I don't agree with it. But I've already tried, and I won't try again."

He shook his father's hand and thanked him, although it hadn't made him feel any better. And it wouldn't make Cassie feel any better either, but he knew he had to go tell her and apologize. Even if she never wanted to speak to him ever again, he owed her that.

TWENTY-ONE

Cassie sat outside under the stars, the flames of the bonfire shooting up into the night. Devastated, she'd spent the afternoon walking along the beach, her mind replaying the events of the day in a loop. She'd been shocked at Alex's cold response to her plea, and that woman—what a piece of work. She'd never met anyone so cold. How they could not understand how important the sanctuary was what boggled her mind.

Now, in the quiet of the night, she just felt exhausted. Taylor had come home with her, and, making sure Cassie would be all right, had gone back to Rancho Del Sol to see Raul. Cassie had insisted she go —hadn't wanted to ruin Taylor's time. At least one of us should have fun, she thought, and she knew Taylor really wanted to have a word or two with Raul. He'd lied, too, and Taylor wanted to call him out on it.

She poked a stick at the glowing logs in front of

her. As the embers floated higher from the fire pit, she noticed movement on the other side, near the house.

She looked over to see Alex striding toward her, his broad shoulders casting a shadow on the sand in the moonlight. Sitting beside her, he reached for her hand. She jumped from her chair, circling to the other side of the fire.

"I don't understand, Alex. Why didn't you tell me who you were? What you were planning? That you were what was standing in the way of the vaquita? I thought we had a connection, and you understood what I stand for." She rammed the stick she was holding into the ground and sat in the sand, waiting for his response.

Alex's face glowed in the firelight. He stared at the flames as his hands worked over the piece of wood in his hands. "I have made a huge mistake, Cassie. I came here to apologize." Dropping the stick, his head sunk heavily into his hands.

Cassie felt her fury quicken, heated by the flames of the fire and the sight of him, so forlorn. "You should have told me from the beginning. Why did you let me go on about the vaquita, let me show them to you? You don't deserve it." She grabbed the stick back out of the ground and rearranged the logs in the fire pit, again sending embers toward the sky.

"If you could just calm down for a moment, I will tell you everything." He stood to his full height, squaring his shoulders, his jaw stronger. Circling the fire pit, he stood close enough to her to reach slowly for the stick she was holding. "I'd prefer if you were unarmed when I do," he said, a slow smile growing. "Will you give me that chance?"

Cassie dropped her eyes to the fire, her hand releasing the stick into his. She felt the warmth of his touch as he took it, her heart softening. "I want to hear everything, Alex. Why did you lie to me?"

Taking a deep breath, Alex sat back down in his chair by the fire. He leaned back, stretching out his legs toward its warmth. "I'm sorry I didn't tell you all of this sooner. I have spent my life being groomed for the position I hold now as CEO for Costa Azul International. My family has been in construction for generations, and I am the only son of my parents, and the only grandson of my grandfather." His hands seemed to have nowhere to rest as he folded his arms across his chest.

"They sent me to the best schools in the United States and spent summers apprenticing under my father. This project here in Rancho Del Sol was to be my debut as CEO of the hotel division of the larger family company, Costa Azul International."

Cassie's eyes grew wide as she made the connection. "Costa Azul International is a huge company, worth millions," she said. "That's your family's company? I thought you just worked for them."

"Yes, it is my family's company, and we have broad holdings," he said, with a wry smile. "My grandfather started with oil and mineral rights and bought all the available property he could decades ago, waiting for the right time to develop it."

"I had no idea," Cassie said, her chin rested on her folded knees. She stared at the fire as she ran back through her memory of this company. The crushing knowledge of the size of her opponent brought heated tears once again.

"My grandfather was fundamentally a kind man, Cassie, but a product of his generation. He wants what's best for his country, for the people of Mexico—and for his family. This particular piece of property, though, is special. It's the only reason emotion is so high surrounding it. I am forbidden to deviate from the plan. It is sacred."

"If he owns half of Mexico, what's so special about this property?" Cassie asked, her brows furrowed now. Her tears had slowed, and her curiosity was getting the best of her.

"This is the part I only found out about tonight. I did not understand why my mother felt so strongly about this piece of property. Many years ago, when I was small, the family suffered a major rift. My mother was not an only child. She had a beloved brother, Pablo, and they were running the business together, with my father and grandfather. It was a group effort, and plans began to develop the property here, in the Baja. It's a beautiful spot, as you know, and my grandfather wanted to help the local economy and provide access to its beauty for all people."

Cassie leaned forward, as Alex's voice had grown soft and low. She waited, as he stared at the flames dancing, the piece of sulphur she had placed in it dripping purple and green.

"Surveying began here, and my Uncle Pablo was in charge of the initial process. He moved to Rancho Del Sol to begin the resort."

"I had no idea anything had been started before. What happened? Why isn't there a 5-star resort there now?" she asked. She began to pace as questions flooded her mind. She had never heard this before, and she thought she knew everything about her local area.

Alex stood also, shoving his hands in his pockets as his voice grew stronger. "My uncle met a woman here. My grandfather is a kind man, as I said, but very traditional in the ways of our culture. The woman was not educated, and their union was forbidden."

"What difference does it make? They were in love," Cassie said softly.

Shaking his head, Alex said, "It meant everything at that time, and I don't think it's as different in your country, Cassie. People don't understand the depth of our traditions. Things are changing slowly, now, but my grandfather would not allow his son to do what he perceived would be throwing his life away."

Her heart fluttered at the pain in Alex's eyes. "Did he ever marry?"

His hands clenching, Alex said, "Pablo defied my grandfather, marrying his love anyway, there on the beach in Rancho Del Sol, before there was a resort of any kind. My grandfather cut him off from the family, both contact and money, and we have never heard from him again." He stood taller now, his amber eyes glowing in the light of the flame.

"Alex, I'm so sorry," Cassie said as she grabbed Alex's hand. "You've heard nothing about him at all, in all these years?"

"My parents heard some stories, but not many. My Uncle Pablo was a master craftsman as well as an expert businessman. They heard he built churches, and later houses, of the ladrillo brick as in this house," he said, gesturing toward Taylor's house behind them. The beautiful arches, with their whale-tail artistry, danced by the light of the fire. "I would be proud of whatever he did."

"He never came back? You never found him at all?" she said, heartache cracking her voice as she spoke.

"My mother was bereft. He was her little brother, and they were very close. She tried to find him once, but my grandfather found out, threatening to banish her and her family from the business as well. From that time forward, we were not allowed to speak of him in my grandfather's presence, and my mother's heart was frozen." He lifted Cassie's hand to his cheek, his touch warming her to her core.

"All I've done my whole life is work, and try to make my family proud, Cassie. I've never been passionate about anything that was my own. It wasn't until I saw you on the beach and had the pleasure of meeting you that I had ever felt drawn to anyone in that way. When I was honored by you sharing your passion for the vaquita, something bigger than any company, that my heart began to beat again."

Alex held Cassie's hand to his lips, gently brushing her palm with his kiss. "By the time I realized you were the person that the company had denied the water rights for the sanctuary, I couldn't bring myself to tell you. I hoped you felt the same way about me, and I didn't want to risk losing you."

She pulled back her hand as if it had touched a flame. "I don't understand. If you're the CEO, why can't you decide about the sanctuary?"

Alex turned and walked toward the cliff. He gazed intently at the beach below and then turned his gaze up toward the stars. "I spoke with my mother earlier. I tried again to persuade her. She knows Pablo was married on that beach, and that's the last place she's ever heard from him. She is intent on leaving it untouched, as a memorial to him. She is immovable on this issue and refuses to speak further of it. She was the one who sent the denial before I'd even seen it."

Cassie gasped, the vision of the cold woman on the dais in front of her. "Your mother?"

"Yes. She believes she is doing the honorable thing

on behalf of her beloved, lost brother. I have not been able to deter her, and I have tried." Turning toward Cassie, he brushed away a wisp of hair blowing in the warm night breeze. "She controls the board, and this afternoon they voted against the sanctuary. I'm so sorry."

Cassie gasped and stepped back, away from him. Alex grabbed her waist, bringing her toward him with one swift pull. Their eyes met, and she looked up at him. He looked as sad as she felt, and she threw her arms around his neck, grabbing tightly.

"I'm so sorry," he said again, and she rested her head on his shoulder.

"I don't know what to do, Alex," she whispered, her warm tears wetting his shirt.

Alex enveloped her in his embrace, rocking her softly. She felt his chin resting on the top of her head as he reached under hers, tilting her face toward the moonlight, toward him. He stood still, his eyes searching hers. Slowly, she stood on her tiptoes, pulling his head toward hers.

His eyes flashed as he leaned into her, his warm lips soft on hers. His arms tightened around her waist as the kiss deepened. Her head spun as she gave her heart to him in a way she never thought she could, to anyone.

He pulled away from her abruptly, his hands still on her waist, making sure she was steady. He stared for a moment at the shadows of the flames flickering on the side of the house. "Whale tails. Master craftsman."

"What are you talking about?" Cassie asked him as she glanced back at the house. It really was beautiful.

Taking a step back, he took her hand. With a slight bow, he said, "I promise I will make it right, Cassie. For you, for the vaquita—and for me."

He brought her hand to his lips once more, lingering for a moment. "Buenos noches, Senorita. We will announce the decision tomorrow at another press conference. At noon. Can I hope to see you there?"

"I wouldn't miss it for the world, Alex." She watched him walk to his Jeep in the moonlight, the coals of the bonfire now turning to ash. She looked out over the water, wondering what he could possibly be able to do now.

TWENTY-TWO

Cassie and Taylor scored a front-row seat after they pushed their way through the throng of reporters standing outside the door. Taylor pulled Cassie through them once again as they heard shouts of, "Any statement, Miss Lewis?" from at least twenty different directions. The commotion left them breathless and they took their seats.

"That was bizarre," Cassie said, turning her head to the back of the room where the photographers covered the doorway. "I feel like Beyoncé or something."

"Well, you don't look like Beyoncé," Taylor said, grinning.

Cassie was grateful to Taylor for the levity, as her heart had been heavy all night. She'd slept fitfully, and morning hadn't come soon enough. The butterflies in her stomach hadn't subsided with daylight, and the program she held in her hands was twisted beyond recognition.

"So, what do you think he's going to do?" Taylor asked, leaning back in her seat and eyeing the dais at the front of the room. It sat empty, with ten minutes until the press conference was scheduled to begin. "Did he actually have a plan last night when he left?"

Cassie had filled Taylor in on Alex's confession earlier that morning. She leaned forward, her hand on Taylor's knee. "I don't know. I have absolutely no idea." She glanced around the room, recognizing many sympathetic faces from the ceremony yesterday, their presence gratifying.

"Do you believe he can fix this?" Taylor said, her eyes full of questions.

"I have absolutely no doubt he will, and I can't quite explain why," Cassie said as her heart warmed with the memory of his touch. His sincerity had moved her, and she utterly believed he would make this right.

"Sounds like you have a lot of faith in him," Taylor said. "And that you're quite smitten again."

"Smitten?" Cassie hadn't heard that word in a long time—particularly in reference to herself. But she had to admit her greatest hope was that he could save her, save the vaquita and would somehow be the man she'd thought he was all a long.

As they waited for the press conference to begin, the room began to fill even more. It hadn't been planned very long, and Cassie noticed the staff scrambling for more chairs. There wouldn't have been time for people to get her from very far away, and her hand covered her mouth as she turned around.

"Taylor, look," she said quietly.

Taylor turned around and gasped. "Oh, my gosh. It's everybody from Playa Luna. Jimmy, Miguel, Mrs. Dayton. Wow. And all your dad's fishing buddies."

Jimmy gave them a thumb's up, and Taylor smiled at Whiskers wagging his tail and looking in the window.

The door behind the dais opened, and the sound of digital camera flashes became almost deafening. Taylor grabbed Cassie's hand as they watched the Board of Directors walk in and take their seats on the platform, its purple velvet cloth in front stamping them with regality. Alex's mother, comfortable in this arena, sat down coolly, turning her gaze directly to Cassie. She smiled slightly, nodding, and turned toward her son as he entered the room.

They both leaned forward as Alex followed the group in a few steps behind. His Armani suit had "business" written all over it, and she had to look twice at him to remember his face as it was last night in the firelight. Searching, she tried to read his expression. Her heart sunk as she realized he wasn't smiling.

The group took their seats, and Alex walked to the podium, blinking as the photographers took picture after picture. "Ladies and gentleman, thank you for joining us today. On behalf of the Board of Directors, I would like to thank those of you who sent messages regarding the vaquita sanctuary. We received all opinions and weighed before coming to a decision."

Alex spoke about the resort again, and the ecosystem surrounding it, and Cassie couldn't help but think he was stalling. His eyes remained steady on the door at the back of the room as he spoke, and she wondered when he would get to the point.

As he ended his overview of the issue, he glanced up hopefully toward the back of the room. His face changed completely, a look of utter relief washing over him. He smiled, his joy obvious as his eyes flashed at what he had spotted.

Turning to the back of the room, Cassie glimpsed Diego standing there, his hands in front of him holding his hat. He smiled at Alex, his expression guarded, as he moved a few steps closer. He was almost unrecognizable to her without his blue jeans, cotton shirt and fishing hat. The hat he held today was that of a Latin gentleman, and the expensive suit he wore made him look like an entirely different man. If she had run into him outside, she wouldn't have known who he was.

She looked back to the dais where Alex's mother was whispering with the woman on her right. She suddenly turned to Alex as the murmurs in the audience grew louder, capturing her attention. She had stopped listening when Alex began to speak of the vaquita, and now, she peered toward the back of the room, shielding her eyes against the bright stage lights the photographers had set up.

"Before I announce the decision of the Board of Directors regarding the water and shore rights for the vaquita sanctuary, I'd like to introduce someone to you. Ladies and gentlemen, it is with great honor I present to you my uncle, Pablo Vasquez."

Taylor's fingernails bit into Cassie's hand and they both gasped as Senora Vasquez jumped to her feet and immediately crashed toward the floor. Alex jumped to his left just in time to catch her before she hit the ground, laying her gently on the carpet. "Water, please," he shouted, as he loosened the pearls around his mother's neck and threw them aside. His uncle and his father arrived at the same time with water, their eyes meeting as they rushed to help the woman they both loved.

TWENTY-THREE

"Clear the room," Alex commanded, gesturing to the assistants in the back. "Raul—" Alex looked around for Raul, but realized he was likely already on his way in search of a first aid kit, as usual.

As they shepherded people out the back door with efficiency, an assistant motioned for Cassie and Taylor to exit with the others.

"They stay here," Alex said, turning back to his mother's side.

Alex wetted a napkin in a glass of water and brushed it lightly across his mother's forehead. Senora Vasquez's eyes fluttered, opening wide as her brother bent over her. Her hand reached toward his face, her palm resting on his check. Tears spilled as she drank in his smile. "Pablo, I never thought I'd see you again. I'd given up all hope."

Alex sat back as Diego—Pablo—gently rubbed his thumb of his sister's cheek.

"I didn't think so either. It wasn't until I saw Alex, here, that my heart allowed me to hope again."

"Pablo, what happened? Why did you leave us?"

"Nina, Father kept us apart in more ways than you know. Even after my wife and son were killed, he wouldn't let me return and inflict shame on the family."

Sitting up, she never let her eyes leave her brother. "Oh, Pablo, you lost Maria? And you had a son?" she wailed, grasping him in a tight hug.

Pablo explained his wife and their young son had been killed in a boating accident. Bereft, he had spent several years building churches and homes in the Baja, lovingly crafting the fire brick structures dotting the landscape.

"It was the way I chose to mourn, Nina. I had to create beauty, as Maria created beauty for me." He held her hand tightly, brushing back her black hair with affection. "I tried to contact you, but father intercepted."

"What? Why would he do that if Maria was gone?" she asked, her knuckles white around Pablo's hand.

"He decided I could come back if I agreed to work again for the company. He insisted it was the only way I could erase the shame. Maria and I had such a quiet life, and to me, her memory was not shameful. I declined, and he forbade me from contact with you and your family." Pablo stood as Nina lowered her eyes and shook her head.

Pablo turned his kind eyes on his brother-in-law, taking him in a warm embrace. Turning to Alex, he said, "And this young man's courage is what brought me here today." He wrapped his arms around Alex, smiling widely. Alex returned the embrace, his eyes bright. "And now that father can no longer stand in our way, there's nowhere else I'd rather be."

Alex nodded. "I couldn't help but replay the story in my mind, of Uncle Pablo's decision to leave the family and marry Maria. I had heard he had built beautiful homes, and when I saw Cassie's house in Playa Luna, I wondered if it had been built by Pablo. Then, after spending the day with him on the water, I wondered if he might be the person we'd lost. I wasn't sure, but took a chance. And now that you're together, the resemblance to Mother is unmistakable." Alex said, taking a seat by his mother.

"He found me last night, at my home. He shared with me your plans not to allow property to be set aside designated for the vaquita sanctuary in an attempt to preserve the beach where we married, in my honor and that of my beloved Maria. I came today to tell you the highest honor to my wife and son would be allowing the sanctuary. If the vaquita survive, that would be something she would have been very proud of."

Cassie's head spun, the shock of seeing Diego as Pablo still rippling through her mind. Alex took her hand, giving it a squeeze. As Cassie squeezed back, Taylor patted Alex on the shoulder. "Way to go, Detective Vasquez," she said, her blue eyes twinkling.

Senora Vasquez stood, leaning on her husband's arm, and crossed the dais. She reached out her hand to Cassie, smiling. "Miss Lewis, it appears you have your sanctuary after all. Would you consider naming it after Pablo and Maria? That would make me very happy."

"It would be an honor, Senora," Cassie said, with a slight nod of her head. "I can't think of anything more wonderful."

Pablo again embraced his sister, his brother-in-law and all the family members on the dais. Alex turned to Cassie, his eyes gentle.

"Ahem," she heard behind her. She turned, and Senora Vasquez motioned to assistants at the back of the room. "Please usher the public back in. We have a vote to take. And I'd like it to be public." With a nod to Cassie, she resumed her seat as the Chairman of the Board of Directors of Costa Azul International.

Cassie held her breath as she stood at the back of the room with her friends from Playa Luna who'd been invited back in. Even the volunteer firefighters had come out, in uniform, and they all hugged her as the board re-assembled on the dais.

A hush fell over the room as Alex stood and stepped over to the podium. "Directors, you are presented with the choice to vote aye or nay on the proposal to donate the previously discussed coastal land and tidewater rights to the Scripps Institute of Oceanography for research and shelter for the vaquita dolphin."

Cassie cleared her throat and caught Alex's eye.

"Porpoise. Excuse me, the vaquita porpoise."

Everyone in the back of the room laughed—they'd all received the porpoise versus dolphin lecture before. As Alex continued to speak, Cassie couldn't take her eyes off of him. He was so assured, so happy, and she couldn't think of a better champion for her—or for the vaquita.

She held her breath again as he called the names of the members and she leaned against Taylor as each member said, in turn, "Aye."

It was unanimous and the room burst into applause. Alex raised his fists in the air and as his mother stared at him with wide eyes, he crossed the dais and kissed her on the cheek, whispering something in her ear. His mother closed her eyes and nodded, standing to give her son a big hug. She turned and smiled in Cassie's direction, nodding at her as well.

"Wow, Cassie, you did it," Taylor whispered as she wrapped her friend in a big hug.

"It wasn't me, it was him," she whispered back. Taylor nodded and looked over toward Alex, who was making a bee-line for Cassie.

"Guess there's more to him than it appeared," Taylor said. She turned to the back of the room, the crowd of friends and neighbors still high-fiving each other.

Cassie nodded slowly, not able to take her eyes off of Alex.

"Come on, everybody, let's wait outside and decide where we're going to celebrate," Taylor said as she winked at Cassie and herded all their friends and neighbors out the back door.

"Cassie, I—"

She raised her finger and put it on his lips. "Sh," she said as she pulled him out a side door and into a hallway decorated with palm trees. She reached her arms around his neck and kissed him, gently but deeply. As she pulled away, her tears spilled and she looked at him with gratitude. He tugged under her chin, tilting her face to his. Her eyes filled with gratitude, she reached up to kiss him once again, the warmth of his lips reaching deep into her heart.

"I don't know how to thank you," she whispered.

"You just did. Perfectly," he said as he leaned in and kissed her again.

"You saved me, Alex. Me and the vaquita."

"If I did, it was for purely selfish reasons. I love you, Cassie. There was no way I was going to lose you. Or let history repeat itself."

Her eyes widened, and she pulled him closer. He rubbed his thumb against her cheek and she closed her eyes. It felt as if she'd always known him, that he would always be there for her.

She stood on her tiptoes to whisper in his ear, "I love you, too."

Cassie tightened her grip on Alex's hand. It was all a miracle—a home for the vaquita and a home for her heart. She'd never in a million years thought she'd be this lucky—or happy.

TWENTY-FOUR

Alex looked out over the crowd still remaining at the press conference. There was a hum of activity still and his mother hadn't let go of his uncle's arm since she'd come to.

"That was a great thing you did in there, Alex. Not just for me, but for them," Cassie said, pointing to the dais.

"Once I had my hunch, I did what I could. Tracked Jimmy down to find Diego—Uncle Pablo— and it was easy from there."

Alex described how he'd gone to Pablo's house to ask him if there were any truth to his suspicion and after Pablo had confirmed the story he'd heard from his mother, they'd taken some time to catch up and make a plan.

"Why so dramatic?" Cassie asked. "You could have

just brought Pablo to your mother now that your grandfather isn't around to object."

"We ended up talking almost all night, and by then it was time for the news conference. If there had been time I would have—but my mother is a very stubborn woman. I wanted to help with the sanctuary also, in addition to re-uniting a brother and sister."

Cassie nodded and squeezed his hand. "Well, it turned out perfectly," she said, standing on her toes to kiss him again. He didn't think he'd ever get tired of that, and he wrapped his arms around her waist and pulled her closer.

"Ahem." Alex's parents and uncle came up behind them and they stepped apart a bit, but Alex kept her hand in his, holding on tightly. He glanced quickly at her and saw her eyes widen as she took a step back. He realized his mother could be difficult and cold, and clearly she'd had a huge impact on Cassie.

"Mother," Alex said, nodding at her as well as his father and uncle.

"That was quite a spectacle," his mother said as she fingered her pearls and eyed Cassie. "Did you know about this?"

"No, no, I was as surprised as you were," Cassie replied with a shake of her head. "Alex and Diego—Pablo—did this all on their own." She lifted her chin and took a step forward. "But I'm glad they did."

Alex swelled with pride at Cassie's courage. His mother could be quite formidable, but Cassie was a fighter through and through, and he loved that about her.

Pablo wrapped his arm around his sister's shoulder, and her face softened in an instant. She tilted her head to rest it on his shoulder, her eyes closed for a moment.

"So am I."

She turned started to head toward the restaurant, and Alex reached out to tap her on her shoulder.

"Mother, I think maybe an apology is in order, don't you?"

She turned, her eyebrows rising before she nodded in Cassie's direction. "Of course."

She took a step toward Cassie and extended her hand. "Please excuse my stubbornness. I thought I was doing the right thing, the honorable thing, for Pablo and Maria after what my father put us through. I couldn't bear that beach where I'd last seen him to be turned into anything—even something so honorable as what you were proposing. I was blinded by history and pain, and I never meant for you—or the dolphin—to suffer."

Cassie opened her mouth and started to say, "They're not—" but Alex tightened his grip on Cassie's hand and she looked up at him, nodded and smiled in agreement that this might not be the best time to have that discussion with his mother. He was impressed that Cassie was getting an apology, and that would have to do for now. He'd make it up to her later.

"Actually, Senora Vasquez, having the sanctuary

be part of the resort is a stroke of genius from a business sense," Raul said as he walked into the hallway, Taylor behind him. "If we turn the resort into more of an adventure site, with kayaking and focus on things that people want to learn more about the Sea of Cortez —and the vaquita—than spend time golfing or playing tennis, we could make this into a world-wide destination. For people who care about the environment, the wildlife."

Alex eyed his mother as she listened to Raul, knowing that her heart and her mind were elsewhere and she was anxious to spend time with her brother, so her response didn't surprise him at all. It was perfect timing.

She waved her hand in Raul's direction. "You've been talking about that for over a year, and it appears that you'll get your wish after all. Why don't the two of you work it out and we can talk about it later. I'm open to anything you want to do, and I'd also like to preserve this property as much as possible. So that it works for everyone, new and old. New visitors and old-time residents alike." She turned to her brother and rested her palm on his cheek.

Turning back to her son, she smiled and nodded again toward Cassie. "Do you think that you could re-evaluate in, say, two weeks? We could have a second ground-breaking with drawings available. I understand it's not enough time for complete re-tooling, but just to unveil an idea?"

Alex turned to Raul, who nodded rapidly. "It appears that we can."

"Good," she said, taking her brother's hand. "We can plan a fiesta, then, and invite all the residents. And that'll give me some time for a little vacation."

Turning to Pablo, she said quietly, "We have some lost time to make up for." She then turned to Cassie. "And some new people to get to know."

TWENTY-FIVE

Cassie looked up, her hand shading her eyes as the Costa Azul International jet circled overhead and landed on the landing strip on the other side of the resort property. She'd grown accustomed to its intermittent presence in the past two weeks, although she wasn't sure she'd ever completely get used to the intrusion in her quiet little world.

As it disappeared behind the dunes, she turned back to the scene of the fiesta they'd worked on. Well, Costa Azul staff had worked on it mostly, as Alex and Raul—and Taylor by phone or Skype—had feverishly drawn up new plans for an utterly transformed resort. During the day, Cassie had done her version of feverish preparations, readying the team who was to prepare— and help manage—the vaquita sanctuary.

Tables with colorful cloths lined the outside of the existing rancho restaurant, which would be transformed into something completely different by the time the resort opened in a year. Opening that soon was a bit optimistic, but by what she'd seen from Alex, Raul, Taylor and the resort team, if anybody could pull it off, they could.

As people from all over the south campos began to arrive—many bringing dishes they'd prepared of tacos, tamales, elotes and grilled fish—Cassie felt Alex behind her, and his arms wrapped around her waist.

"Where have you been?" Cassie asked as she turned to him, realizing he was out of breath.

"I had a small thing to attend to. It's all sorted out now." He glanced at the tables and frowned. "This wasn't supposed to be a potluck. It was a gift and a celebration from us," he said. They both watched people arrive, set down their dishes next to the caterers and eagerly go to see the new plans—for both the resort and the vaquita sanctuary—that were set up on easels under colorful tarps. The sea sparkled in the distance and Cassie couldn't remember a time when so many people she'd known since she was a child had come together with such excitement and anticipation.

"We don't even get this many people out for the annual Fireman's Fiesta."

"Is that a fundraiser?" he asked, stepping up beside her and taking her hand.

"Yes, we do it ever year," she said as she waved at Colin, who proudly wore his fireman's uniform. "The locals and Americans banded together years ago, and

Colin was the lead organizer. They've gotten fire trucks donated from both countries and have saved multiple homes."

Alex sounded surprised when he said, "There are many fires here?"

Cassie nodded. "Mostly from runaway fireworks on New Year's Eve or Easter. Taylor's brother loved fireworks but as far as I can tell, never started a fire."

"Ah," he said as he pulled her back toward the restaurant, glancing anxiously toward the parking lot.

"No, I didn't."

Cassie spun at the familiar voice, and let out a laugh as Taylor's brother, Kyle, hugged her and lifted her toes out of the sand.

"Kyle, what are you doing here?" she said, out of breath from the bear hug she'd just gotten."

"Well, I got a break from my residency when I heard there was going to be a celebration and we didn't want to miss it."

"We?" Cassie said, her breath hitching as he turned around and pointed behind him.

Cassie's eyes welled up at the sight of her mother. She rushed toward her and flung her arms around her neck.

"Hello, sweetheart," her mother whispered in her ear. "I'm so, so proud of you."

"Mom, I—I just don't know what to say. I can't believe you're here," Cassie said as she brushed away a tear. She hadn't seen her mother in months and had wished she'd been able to be there for the vaquita presentation and now—here she was. "How—what—"

Taylor's mother Felicia stepped up and gave her a hug, too, with Taylor beaming from behind her.

"We got an offer we couldn't refuse," Taylor said. She pointed at Alex. "This guy sure knows how to treat your family right. We had quite an interesting trip on the private jet."

Cassie's eyes widened and she turned to Alex, who looked quite pleased with himself. "I couldn't help it. I knew you'd want them here for the ground-breaking. It wouldn't be a celebration without family. All of our family."

He turned and looked down to the beach, where his mother and his Uncle Pablo walked slowly with their toes in the water, talking non-stop as they had been for almost two weeks now. Senora Vasquez was almost unrecognizable from when Cassie had first met her, in her Chanel suit and pearls. Now, her dark hair flowed over her shoulders and her long, brightly colored skirt fluttered over her bare feet.

Cassie's joy spread all the way to her own toes, and she grabbed her mother's hand. "Oh, I need introduce you all," she said.

"We met earlier at the air strip," Megan said. "Quite an amazing man you have here, Cass."

Cassie looked around at her family—her old family and her new one—and knew her mom was right. Between all these people who loved her and her vow to the vaquita, her world was bright, and looked brighter by the day.

"I'm so happy for you, Cassie," Megan said. "It's like a dream come true."

Cassie looked up into her mother's eyes. Her breath hitched a bit—her mom had dark circles under her eyes and although she was clearly happy for Cassie, she looked tired.

"Are you all right?"

Her mom nodded. "Sure. I'm just a little short on sleep. Running the girls' home is a little rough sometimes. All worth it, mind you, but rough."

"Mom, are you sure this is right for you? I want you to be as happy as I am."

Megan laughed. "Well, aside from the fact that I'm past the boyfriend stage, it's what Erica and I always said we wanted to do. We need to give it the old college try, right?"

"Sure. But please be open. I'd love it if you could come here with me, watch the sanctuary and the resort grow. Maybe be a grandma."

Cassie blushed as her mother nodded and smiled as her mother dropped a light kiss on her cheek."

"I know this is where you're supposed to be. I know you and Alex will be happy here. Don't you worry about me. I just want you to be happy."

Cassie caught Alex's eye and smiled as he waved from the tents and showed the press the drawings of the new resort and the plans of the sanctuary—the sanctuary she'd not long ago given up hope for.

She thought of how close she had come to believing he would never give it all up for his family. She knew now that he was her rock, her rescuer, and she could rest her heart in his hands and not take on the world alone. She was overwhelmed with gratitude as she turned to the sea, to her sanctuary. "Yes, we will be happy here."

"Whiskers," Megan said, jumping up and rushing to give Whiskers a pet and Jimmy a hug.

"Hi, Megan. Nice to see you all here for the fireworks," Jimmy said as he greeted his old friends.

"Did somebody say fireworks?" Kyle asked, looking up at the sky.

"No, no fireworks, Kyle." Alex shook his head.

"Well, that's too bad," Kyle said as he and Taylor headed toward the displays and food tables. "Come on, let's get this party started. There's a lot to celebrate."

Alex cleared his throat. "I know you all just arrived, but would you mind if I steal Cassie for just a moment? We'll be right back."

Cassie thought she saw him wink at her mother, but that couldn't be. They'd just met.

"What is it, Alex?" she asked.

"Just come with me. I want to show you something."

"Sorry," she called over her shoulder to her family

as they headed toward a table in the shade and the mariachis began playing.

"We're fine," Megan said. "Take your time."

"What's going on?" Cassie asked again as he started the Jeep and headed away from the ocean, circling a bit south of the resort property and climbing up to a cliff overlooking the ocean. He hadn't answered either time, so she decided she'd just go along for the ride. He hadn't steered her wrong yet, and she trusted that this, too, would be worth it.

As he pulled to a stop atop a cliff overlooking the sparkling sea, he hopped out and opened her door, extending his hand.

"Come with me," he said, his eyes twinkling.

She followed him, and the warm breeze on her skin calmed her. She knew she was safe, and the warmth in her heart told her that she could trust him with anything.

TWENTY-SIX

Alex's nerves were a bit frazzled after the frenzy of the past couple of weeks, re-evaluating the resort and planning a party. But he was pleased with the outcome—Taylor had been a big help, Raul was really in his element, and what they'd come up with would be very unique. He truly knew of nothing like it anywhere.

And coordinating the arrival of Cassie's mother had been a bit of a challenge, but Taylor had helped a lot. When he'd finally called her mother to introduce himself and tell her what he had planned, they'd had a very nice—even lengthy—conversation, after which she'd thanked him for the opportunity and promised secrecy about the trip—and for what was about to come next. He'd enjoyed their conversation and realized that he liked her a great deal, not surprised at all that Cassie's mother was quite an interesting, insightful person like Cassie herself.

He took in a deep breath and pulled Cassie over to the center of a large concrete slab that he'd had poured, hoping that all went well.

"What is this, Alex?" Cassie asked as he stopped her in the center of the slab and turned her toward the sea.

"What do you see?"

"Oh," she said, her hand on her heart. "This is the most perfect view of the sanctuary I've ever seen. It's—it's right in front of us and up this high I can see the whole thing. Well, what will be the whole thing. It's beautiful."

Alex stepped in front of her and took her hands in his. "Yes, beautiful," he echoed, but he wasn't looking at the sea. He was looking into the eyes of his friend, his compatriot, his partner in crime. He'd known she was special from the moment he'd crashed through the waves to save her, and he knew it even more so now.

He waved his hand over the concrete. "What do you think about it for a site for a house? Big, plate glass windows here overlooking the beach and the sanctuary —and over here, to see the resort."

"It's lovely," she said. "And a kitchen right here, with the sink looking to the south."

Alex laughed at how she guessed at where he'd planned to put the sink, and he couldn't wait to show her the plans Pablo had drawn up for it. But he had something more important to do first.

He reached behind a small bush, pulled out a glass

box and held it in front of her, smiling at her expression.

"Oh, Alex, the Murex."

She took the box from him and opened it, gently lifting out the shell she'd almost drowned over, never letting go of it. "I wondered what happened to it. You kept it."

"I did. I didn't want to ever let it or you go, to be honest. It's been on my nightstand all this time and it's the last thing I see when I go to bed."

Color crept into her cheeks, and he smiled as she put it up to her ear and then shook it.

"Oh, I thought I made sure it didn't have anything living in it," she said with a frown. "I hope I wasn't wrong. Something's rattling."

Knowing she'd be devastated if she thought she'd killed something, he took the shell from her and reached for her hand, shaking out the contents into her palm. He took in a deep breath, hoping that all would go as planned.

He let his breath out when her eyes grew wide as she looked at the diamond ring he'd picked out. And he was able to breathe in again when she smiled and looked up at him, her eyes wet as she blinked against the sun.

"Alex?"

He bent down on one knee and reached for her other hand. "Cassie, will you marry me? Live here with me in this house we build for us, and help me make this place even more special than it already is?"

Cassie nodded slowly, put the ring on her finger and sat on his knee. She wrapped her arms around him and rested her palm on his cheek, the diamond sparling in the sun.

"Alex, you've created my dream come true, in more ways than one. I can't think of anything—and I mean anything—that would make me happier," she said.

He pulled her toward him and rested his lips on hers, the sweet salt of her tears making him the happiest man alive.

I HOPE YOU ENJOYED As DEEP As THE OCEAN!

The next book,
As Bright As the Stars,
features Megan's mom, Cassie, and the poaching and smuggling of an endangered deep water fish, the totoaba.
If you'd like to receive an email when the book releases, please join my mailing list.

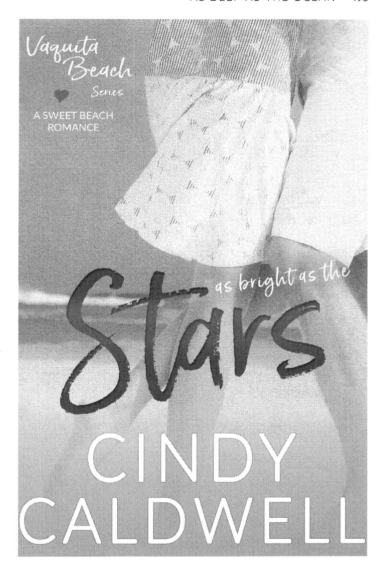

Vaquita
Beach
Series

A SWEET BEACH
ROMANCE

as bright as the

Stars

CINDY
CALDWELL

ABOUT THE AUTHOR

Cindy Caldwell writes heartwarming stories interwoven with the bonds of friendship and family that combine what she loves most about women's fiction and romance.

Cindy lives in and loves everything about the southwest, from its deserts and mountains to the sea. She discovered her passion for writing after a twenty-year career in education. When she's not writing, she travels as much as she can with her children who, although adults, still need her no matter what they think.

Feel free to sign up for her list to hear about new releases as soon as they are available as well as extras like early bird discounts. Just cut and paste into your browser: http://eepurl.com/bYAZEL

46194897R00111

Made in the USA
Lexington, KY
24 July 2019